Valuable Pain:

Money, Lies, and Heartbreak

By: Kyeate

STAY CONNECTED

Facebook: Kyeate TheAuthor/ Kyeate Holt

Facebook Group: Kyewritez & Thingz

Instagram: Kyewritez

You got to know where we came from to understand where we are.

CHAPTER 1
Niara Pines

Early Years: 2015

The moment was bittersweet yet satisfying because I was one step closer to my dreams. Today I had completed my final hours of cosmetology school. The only thing left was to take my state board test and open my salon. It sounded easy in my head, but I knew if it weren't for my grandmother and uncle, this would've been an even longer journey.

When I graduated high school, I didn't immediately go to college because I wasn't sure what I wanted to do. My mother pointed straight at the door and told me to leave since she felt that I was throwing my life away. That's where my grandmother and my Uncle Rodney came in at. Moving in with my granny gave me free rein with my life. She respected the fact that I was trying to find myself. It wasn't like I was a troubled teen or anything. I wasn't one of those girls that were running the streets or came from a broken home. My family was well off. Even though most of the money came from my uncle and his kingpin ways, they made sure that I made something out of myself, so they supported me.

I placed my flat irons and other items in my suitcase. I was tired as hell and couldn't wait to get home and soak my ass in the tub. I moved out of my granny's a month after I enrolled in school. At twenty-four years old, my life was peaceful, drama-free with no kids, so I had no complaints with the pace that I was moving.

"Bihhhh yass, it's official, we up out this thang and one step closer to our dreams!" Kima squealed.

Kima and I had met here at school and been kicking it ever since. We had become close because just like me. She didn't respond well to other females, and somehow, we clicked. I wouldn't say Kima was ratchet, but she was the loud, down for whatever, rambunctious chick. Even through all of that, she was a hustler and about her paper. Over the months leading to our graduation, we had mapped out a whole business and decided we would go into business with each other by opening our salon.

Turning around, I threw my arms around her.

"Yes, it's over, hoe."

"I know you coming out with me tonight to celebrate. Plus, it's my brother's birthday and he done closed down the whole club for his party," she rambled.

Even though I wanted to say hell no, I could tell how excited she was, so what the hell.

"Yes, I'll go, Kima." I sighed.

Kima jumped up and down and grabbed ahold of her roller suitcase. I grabbed mine, and we headed out the door.

"So listen, I'm going to come to your house bout nine so that we can pre-game. Bitch, don't half step either. Your ass is gone get you a man tonight. The dust that virgin coochie holds needs to be knocked off." Kima laughed.

All I did was shake my head and flick her the bird. She was always trying to hook a bitch up with somebody. And to make matters worse, yes, I was a virgin, but that was my decision. These niggas here wasn't worth the secretions that slid out of me.

On my drive home, I was going over in my head something to wear to the club. I ain't gone lie. The thought of maybe meeting someone sounded good as fuck to me. Being a virgin was my business, and I'm slick glad that I was because the men that I had encountered over the years in which I called myself dating was full of shit. Typically, when you meet a guy, you get at least three months of bliss before the bullshit hits, but these days with the guys here in the city that shit was null and void.

Pulling up to my apartment, I parked in my spot and removed my things from the car, making my way into the house. Unlocking the door, I stepped in and kicked off my shoes right there at the door. It was nothing like home. Removing my smock, I started to undress and headed straight to the shower. Once the jets from the shower hit my body, it sent vibrations through me that soothed my tense body. The Dove anti-stress body wash did its job as I lathered my body several times and rinsed off. Kicking the water off, I grabbed my towel and wrapped it around my body.

Sitting on the bed, I reached into my nightstand and removed my special box. Opening it up, I removed a pre-rolled blunt and lit it. Letting the smoke fill my lungs, I grabbed my phone and scrolled through my social media. Coming across Kima's page, I saw a flyer for her brother's party and read over it. It was a picture of him, and it was my first time seeing him. This motherfucker was fine as hell— no wonder she been holding out.

A text came through, breaking me from my thoughts. It was Kima.

Kima: *Bitch. Don't flake and get ready to make that ass shake.*

Me: *Girl, fuck you. I'm not flaking.*

Kima: *See you soon.*

Me: *Aite.*

Tossing the phone, I hopped out of bed and headed to my closet. Looking at the many different pieces of clothing I had, I wanted to look sexy but still classy. I wasn't about to go in here looking like no fucking thot. I opted for this jade green sequin wrap dress that had a deep V cut in the front and a pair of gold and black, strappy stilettos. Laying my outfit across my bed, I headed to the bathroom to start on my hair and makeup.

***

Kima and I pulled up at Midtown Lounge, and the crowd was thick as fuck. We parked and got out. Kima handed her keys to valet as we made our way inside. The clicking of cameras caught me off guard because I was high as fuck from the blunts we had smoked during our pre-game session.

"Bitch, your brother is that big he's got a red carpet at his party?" I joked.

"Nash always says go big or don't even do that shit." Kima laughed.

We stopped and posed for a few pictures. I was feeling myself. I had done my hair in a high ponytail that was bone straight. My makeup was flawless, and I just knew my shit was on point. Kima adorned some black bell-bottom slacks that hugged her ass like paint, which was complemented with a sheer gold bralette. Her makeup on her bronze color skin gave her a glow. We were about to be the baddest things up in here.

Walking in, we headed straight to the bar. I felt someone tug at my arm. That right there alone pissed me off, and then I realized when turning around it was Kima.

"Bitch, we got a section and don't have to pay for shit," she said, pointing towards the upstairs level. I nodded my head and followed her.

The crowd was everything, and I was impressed with the turnout. We bopped through the crowd to the sounds of Future's "March Madness" as it blasted through the speakers, and the crowd broke out in an uproar. We made it upstairs and bitch I thought I had died and gone to heaven. It looked like straight money up in this bitch. I was never thirsty for a nigga with money because I was well off, but my ass broke out in a coughing fit, dying for something for my thirst to be quenched. *My thirsty ass.* Kima looked back at me.

"You good?" she asked with her face all screwed up.

"I need something to drink," I gasped.

Kima walked over to another small booth across from the guys where there sat a girl alone sipping and bopping to the music.

When she saw Kima approaching, she smiled and hopped up.

"Kima!" she yelled.

Kima embraced her while I looked back over my shoulders and all eyes were on my ass. Turning back around, Kima excitedly introduced me to the girl.

"Niara, this is Desire. This is the wife of my brother's best friend."

I smiled and hugged her.

Niara handed me a cup, and I gave it a sniff. I wasn't sure what it was, but I knew it was strong as hell. I threw the drink back and let the liquid warm me up. I turned around, and my eyes locked on him. Kima's brother was staring a hole in me. I looked off and looked back, and he was still looking at me. Shit, he had me thinking we had beef.

The way he was looking at me wasn't pleasant or lustful. His eyes were dark, but other than that, I couldn't help but admire how fine he was in person. The presence he gave off wasn't warm or welcoming. His skin was the color of ground cinnamon. He rocked a low-cut fade, which was trimmed to perfection. His small beard was perfect and not taking away from his facial features. The thickness of his brows furrowed as he nodded his head while another guy was talking to him. I didn't know who he was, but he looked like the rapper Dave East.

I took another sip of another drink Kima had handed me and when the DJ had the nerve to mix in Future's "Freak Hoe", I lost it. This was my shit, and I started rapping the lyrics like I was bout that life. I got lost in the song and in my head as if nobody was in the room but me.

"Damn sis, you walk in this bitch, come in a nigga's section, drink my liquor, but don't even tell me happy birthday," I heard his voice boom.

Kima hugged her brother, and the other guy who I now know was his best friend because he came over and wrapped his arms around Desire and nodded his head at Kima. I continued to dance and rap the lyrics with so much spunk.

"Who is you? I know you ain't bout that life," I heard him whisper in my ear as he took a sip out the bottle he was holding. The smell of mint and liquor only smelt pleasant coming from him.

I bit my lip, and I don't know what came over me, but I gazed at him seductively.

"I'm Niara, a friend of Kima's. If you have to ask who I am, you wouldn't know what I'm about!" I snapped.

I was in my head cheering myself on as if this nigga wasn't putting fear in my panties. He was that damn fine, like scared to give him the pussy fine.

"Hell no, I said find a nigga but not this one. He's off-limits!" Kima stepped in between the both of us.

"Man, bruh, move around. I'm just asking shorty her damn name!" Nash spat, shoving Kima out the way.

Kima gave me that look like *please don't* and went back to drinking. I don't know what the look was for and why she was blocking, but I figured it was for a reason. Kima walked over to another guy that was with them and started talking. Hopefully, he kept her occupied because I felt myself finna flirt with Nash all night.

CHAPTER 2
Nashville "Nash" Palero

A nigga had made it to see twenty-four, and I was throwing the biggest party in the Ville for that shit. It slick was a blessing each birthday I shared because it was tough out here. It was nobody but my sister Kima and me, and I refused to leave her out here alone.

I started working for this cat name Rodney when I was sixteen, and since he stepped down, he remained my plug, but I took over. Rodney used to fuck around with my mama back in her heyday, and my ass was wilding one day robbing a corner market so I could feed Kima and me. When I ran out of the store, I bumped into him. After lifting me by my collar, the nigga asked was I Peaches' boy. I nodded my head yes in fear because I knew exactly who he was. After he carried my ass back in the store, in which he owned, he asked me why I was out here in the streets, and I told him everything. I'd been working for him ever since.

As I moved up in rank on the streets, people saw that I wasn't to be messed with. My name was me, and it spoke on who I was— Nashville. I owned this damn city. When I was younger, I couldn't believe my mama named me fucking Nashville. Talking bout, she ain't know my daddy. She just knew he was the first nigga she fucked when she moved to Nashville. That's why I went by Nash. The ladies loved that shit too. Money was top priority, Kima, and then pussy.

My homies Fiyah and AB and I stood in the VIP section looking over the club. It was lit as hell in here tonight, and I was drinking Hennessey straight out the bottle. I peeped when my sister walked in, and I already wanted to go in her shit with that skimpy ass shirt she had on. Shorty that was trailing her caught my eye as well. She was rocking the hell out a green dress the same color as the Versace button-down that I was rocking. When they made it up the steps, they walked over to Desire. I ain't even take my eyes off her.

"Nigga, did you hear what the fuck I said?" Fiyah spat.

I nodded my head but never took my eyes off shorty. I could tell she was uncomfortable because she was fidgeting like a motherfucker and kept drinking.

"Yeah, I heard your ass. I'm trying to figure out who shorty is tho." I licked my lips and adjusted the chain I had around my neck. Fiyah leaned in to look at what had my eye.

"She's a decent piece. She don't look like she on that ratchet shit like Kima." He laughed.

I looked at this nigga like he was crazy. I knew my sister was ratchet, but that wasn't his place to call it.

"Get off Kima, dog," AB interrupted. That nigga thought I didn't know he had a thing for her, but I did.

"Freak Hoe" came on, and all that classy shit went out the window. Ole gal started twerking and rapping word for word, so I made my ass over that way. I spit a few words to my sister then made my way to her. I felt the conversation could've gone further if Kima hadn't brought her blocking ass back over here. Niara was her name, and I was trying to see what she was talking about. I needed some new birthday pussy.

The night was moving smoothly, and the drinks were flowing. A nigga was feeling real good. The girls were drunk as hell and on that drunk punk shit standing on couches and shit, but we were balling and showing our ass tonight.

"Y'all put ya drinks in the air and let's give a toast to the birthday boy and king of the city Nashville. To y'all motherfuckers he's Nash. I've been knowing that nigga since he was a youngin' so I can call him that. This one is for you, homie!" the DJ yelled in the mic and then dropped my favorite damn song, Meek Mill's "Dreams and Nightmares".

When the beat kicked in, I held my diamond bezel Nash chain that I had around my neck up. I had that shit custom made. I rapped the words to the song and let that shit hit my soul.

"Nash, you really not gone let me in!" I heard this nagging ass voice coming from the left of me.

I opened my eyes mad as hell that somebody was fucking up the vibe I had going. When I looked over, I saw the lil chick I had dropped dick off in and wasn't even checking for her ass no more.

"Hoe, move around." I hit her with a head nod and went back to my song.

When I looked back at Niara, she had taken a seat on the couch and looked like she was about done. I laughed, fucking lightweight.

A nigga had to take a piss, so I set the bottle down and made my way downstairs. Walking through the crowd, I was giving out daps, hugs, and squeezing ass here and there. This other little baddie that I used to fuck was standing at the bar, and her eyes lit up when she saw a nigga. She made her way towards me.

"Happy Birthday, Nash," she whispered in my ear and ran her hand over my dick. I looked down at her thick ass.

"What you got for me?" I asked, getting straight to the point.

"Shit, what you want?" she replied.

I grabbed her hand and pulled her towards the bathroom. Walking inside, I checked underneath all the stalls making sure it was clear. Reaching into my pocket, I pulled out a hundred-dollar bill and handed it to the attendant.

"Make sure nobody comes in here," I demanded. He nodded his head and walked out. Ole girl bent over lifting her dress, leaning on the sink.

"Nah, I want some head," I smirked.

"I'm not putting my knees on this nasty ass floor," she smacked, instantly killing my vibe. Dammit, all a nigga needed was something wet, but I just wanted that top right now.

"Suit yourself." I shrugged and walked back out of the bathroom, bumping into Niara.

"Damn, my bad," I said, catching her fall.

When she looked up and saw me, she smiled until she saw ole gal come out of the bathroom behind me. She had the nerve to snatch her arms out of my hand. *Oh, she jealous, huh.* I winked my eye as she stomped in the bathroom. I thought about my next move, and I looked at the attendant again. All he did was nod his head, and I eased in the bathroom.

I leaned up against the sink while Niara was in the bathroom, pissing. She was cussing, and I placed my hand over my mouth, laughing at her drunk ass.

"Never get drunk and squat in stilettos. This shit ain't right," she said to no one.

The toilet flushed, and after a few moments, she walked out. When she saw me standing there, her mouth dropped. Shit, she was even better looking in the light, drunk and all. Shorty looked mixed with something. She gave me exotic vibes, from her warm cappuccino skin and light brown eyes. She looked at me with her light brown eyes, which were round and stood out. She ain't have to wear them fake ass lashes because hers was thick and curled up.

"You good?" I sized her up, breaking the silence. She walked over to the sink, bit down on her pouty lips, and started to wash her hands. I don't know what she had on, but her scent was driving me crazy. I couldn't help but run my fingers through her ponytail.

"This your real hair?"

"Yes, you probably used to bald head hoes!" she snapped.

Scratching my beard, I let out a little laugh.

"I ain't think you cared."

"Trust me. I don't. I don't even know you."

She started to walk out, and I grabbed her arm, pushing her up against the wall. We stood nose to nose, and she quickly turned her head to break our gaze.

"Look at me," I demanded, grabbing her face. Her breathing had become labored.

"I want you after the club," I flat out said. Slipping my hands underneath her dress, I could feel the heat radiating off that pussy.

"Kima is not about to kill me," she whispered.

I knew I had her once I inserted my finger in that shit, and she was tight as a motherfucker. I watched as a moan escaped her lips, and her eyes rolled back. Finally, she looked at me with that look she gave me earlier. She rode that wave for a hot little minute. I guess till she came to her senses.

"I got to go. This isn't right," she said quickly slapping my hand from underneath her dress.

She was moving fast as hell out the bathroom. She was moving so fast that she didn't realize something fell out of her clutch. Bending down, I picked it up and smiled as I looked at her driver's license. This night was far from over.

CHAPTER 3

Niara

This damn liquor had taken over my body. I couldn't believe I stood there and let him do that shit to me. Don't get me wrong. That shit felt good, but Kima would kill me. I texted Kima and told her that I was sick and was catching an Uber home. She was going to breakfast with AB, and I wanted no parts of it.

When I finally made it through the crowd and outside, my Uber was waiting for me. Looking back over my shoulder, I could see Nash slowly coming through the crowd. I didn't know if he was following me or not, but I had to go. Getting in the car, my driver pulled off and headed to my crib. Grabbing a bottle of water that they had sitting in the backseat, I gulped that shit down so fast. I needed my ass smacked for drinking like I did tonight. Overall, I had a good time.

Flashes of Nash kept popping up in my head, he had moved something in me, and now I wished I hadn't of stop him. I could still feel his fingers inside of me. Biting down on my lip, I shook those thoughts from my head as we pulled up at my apartment.

'Thank you," I told the Uber driver as I slowly exited the car. Looking into my clutch, I grabbed my door key.

"Niara!" I heard my name being called. I know this wasn't this nigga.

I slowly turned around, and Nash was standing in the cut, looking like a damn stalker. He walked into the light with a slight smirk on his face as he made his way towards me.

"I didn't take you as the stalking type. Were you following me?" I snapped with a frown fixed on my face even though I was glad to see his ass.

"Ma, what did I tell you in the bathroom? Oh, you thought I was playing, shorty?" he spoke in a serious tone as he closed the gap between us.

"Plus, I figured you needed this," he said, looking down it was my driver's license.

Snatching the license from his hand, I turned on my heels and headed towards my apartment. I knew he was behind me. Lord, what the hell was about to happen?

Unlocking the door, we entered my apartment, and I headed straight towards my bedroom. I was ready to get out of these shoes. He could stay for a little bit because I know he had been drinking, and he doesn't need to drive. Yeah, that sounded like a reasonable explanation.

I felt his presence standing in the doorway of my bedroom. Slowly I took him in. I didn't notice all the tattoos in the club, but I could see them now.

"Go take a shower, shorty," he demanded. His voice was calm, but I knew he meant that shit.

I couldn't believe I got up as fast as I did. Damn near busting my ass tripping over the rug, I hopped up and went to handle my business. Lord, from the looks of Nash I knew he wasn't a stranger to getting pussy. At the same time, I wanted this, but I was scared as hell. I felt a slight breeze come into the bathroom, and Nash stood there naked as the day he was born. Scanning his body, when my eyes landed on that third leg, I was not about to fuck this man.

Swallowing the lump that formed in my throat, I couldn't even formulate a sentence. Nash entered the shower, and his hands started to roam my body slowly.

On contact, I closed my eyes as he planted kisses on my

neck. This was so wrong but felt so right. Nash turned me around and placed my hands on the shower wall. I could feel him rubbing his dick up and down my entrance. Oh my god, I needed to tell him I was a virgin because if this nigga slipped inside of me full force, he was going to be in for a surprise.

"I'm a virgin," I whispered, anticipating his next move. He stopped rubbing against my clit.

"What?" he mumbled.

"I'm a virgin," I repeated. Nash held his head down in defeat.

"How old are you again?" he asked, running his hand over his face.

"I'm twenty-four. Excuse me for not being polite with my pussy!" I snapped. He had made me mad that quick. I grabbed a towel and stepped out of the shower.

"You need to get dressed so you can leave," I told him and walked back in the bedroom.

He had me fucked up, questioning me as if I was lying about something so important. Kima was right, and I could see where she came from when she said what she said. Nash made his way out of the bathroom.

"Yo, you forreal right now?

"Nash, just go. This ain't what you want." I shrugged. Making his way over to me, Nash dropped his towel.

"I guess I have to show you what I want then." He smiled.

This motherfucker was so damn sexy. I wasn't sure if the water was rolling off my body from the shower or if I was just that damn wet. He made his way between my legs and snatched my towel from around me.

"Lay back," he demanded, and I complied.

What came next shocked the hell out of me. Now, I have had my pussy ate before, and I sucked my share of dick here and there, but for Nash to do this shit, I knew he was about to have my head gone. The way his thick tongue glided like it was on a slippery slope, I couldn't contain myself. Placing my hand on his head, he gazed up at me with evil eyes.

"Do I need to tie your hands up? Keep your hands above your head," he voiced, then he went right back to feasting on my throbbing pussy. When Nash shot off demands, that shit turned me on.

Since I couldn't touch him, I grind my shit in his face as hard as I could. Dipping his fingers in my shit, I could tell he was inserting more each time he dipped in.

"Fuck, I can't take this shit no more," he groaned. Placing his body between my legs, he looked down at me.

"Look, I ain't finna front and tell you this shit ain't gone hurt. I don't know how long it will be until it feels pleasurable for you. I'm a bit rough at times, but I guess since I'm your first, I can take it easy. You sure you want to do this, and please know that I'm a single man and nothing will come from this." He sighed.

Hold the fuck up, did I miss something. How the hell he just finna lay some rules and he taking my damn virginity?

"Just come on." I sighed. Hell, I just wanted some dick right now, specifically his dick.

Using his thumb, he toyed with my pearl some more then he spat on my shit for some reason that drove me wild, and then he slid right in.

"Fuckkkk!" I yelled out as my body went through some things trying to adjust to this contraption that he called a dick.

My body was reacting to him, even though this shit was painful as hell. Once I felt myself rocking with him, it was murder I fucking wrote.

CHAPTER 4

Fiyah

"Dad, can you please get up and make Ashlyn get ready?" I heard my son Ashton's voice whining in my ear.

This little nigga here, I was gone get in his ass for whining like a little ass girl. I peeked my eye opened, and he was standing there with his arms crossed, and Ashlyn was sitting in the floor behind him ass naked. I used my other hand and felt for Desire, and she wasn't there. A nigga's head was banging from all that damn drinking.

"Dad!" Ashton yelled again.

"Dammit boy, where's yo mama's ass at?" I huffed. Sitting up, I threw the covers off me and sat on the edge of the bed.

"She said she was making breakfast and for you to get your ass up and help me," Ashton said repeating everything she had said.

I ran my hands over my face and shook my head.

"What I tell you about that damn cussing?" I spat. Ashton was my son I had with Nessa. I got when he was five, and now at seven, his ass just sprouted.

"I was just telling you exactly what Ma Desi said." He shrugged, rolling his eyes. I laughed because that was his nickname he came up with for Desire after we took him in. He knew Desire wasn't his mom, but after I had to get rid of Nessa's ass, Desire stepped in.

I got out of bed, walked over to Ashlyn, and scooped her

naked ass up. She was my pride and joy. It was crazy that she was a product of Desire and me. I carried her out of the room and headed to her bedroom. Desire had laid her clothes out for the day.

Holding up the shirt, I asked her, "Ashy, can you put this on for daddy?"

Ashlyn stuck out her lip and shook her head no. For two years old, she was smart as a whip, running behind her brother. See, this was why Desire ass needs to be up here. I sighed and laid the clothes back down. I opened the drawer and pointed to it.

"You find you something to wear." Ashlyn ran to the drawer and started pulling clothes out. I walked out and peeked into Ashton's room

"Keep an eye on your sister while I get dressed," I told him. I walked back into the bedroom and stepped into the bathroom. Looking in the mirror, I removed the durag I had, showing off my braids. I don't know what the hell prompted me to grow my hair out, but I could rock anything.

Over the years, things have been going well once we removed all the dead weight from our lives. I expanded, and we had a funeral home in Memphis and Atlanta. A nigga still had his hand in illegal dealings, but it is what it is.

After washing my face and cleaning my pearly whites, I jumped in the shower. Closing my eyes, I thought about the session Desire, and I had last night after the club, immediately my dick rocked up. I massaged my dick so that I could get a quick nut out because I knew Desire's ass. If she was dressed for work already, that shit was out the question.

"Fiyah, why in the hell is my child dressed like this!' Desire yelled busting up in the bathroom. I opened my eyes and still had my dick in my hand. I turned my back towards her and Ashlyn.

"Damn Desire, can't you knock?" I asked.

"Go sit on the bed," she told Ashlyn. I rinsed the soap off my body.

"I know you weren't up in here jacking off with your nasty ass?" she asked. I looked at Desire and bit my bottom lip.

"Let me get a quickie then?" Desire rolled her eyes.

"No, I have to be at the funeral home in twenty minutes and still drop the kids off. I asked you to get Ashlyn dressed," she grunted as she fixed her hair in the mirror. Stepping out the shower, I wrapped the towel around my waist.

"That girl is a drama queen like your ass. She ain't like that shit you laid out, so I let her pick what she wanted to wear," I told Desire as I walked up behind her and placed my dick on her ass. She closed her eyes, and a moan escaped her lips.

"Stop, now I have to get her dressed, or I'm going to be late. Your breakfast is downstairs, and it's a plate wrapped up for AB's hungry ass too," Desire said as she pushed me off her using her ass.

I watched as she grabbed Ashlyn and was saying something to her as they walked out of the room. I proceeded to get dressed in my attire for the day. Ain't nothing changed. It was all black for me today. Desire tried to get me to switch it up over the years, but I couldn't do it.

After getting dressed, I headed downstairs to the kitchen and smashed the breakfast that Desire had made. Desire made her way into the kitchen with Ashlyn and Ashton on her heels.

"Bye, baby I'll see you at the funeral home," she said, planting a kiss on my cheek. I leaned down, kissed Ashlyn, and dapped up Ashton as I watched my family leave out the kitchen. It was no better feeling than having a family. I thought I would never see the day I Fiyah Cole became a family man.

AB

"Damn girl," I moaned, holding the back of Kima's head. Kima was doing her thang on her knees.

See, shit like this I could get used to. I was on my way out of the door to meet up with Fiyah, but Kima pulled my ass back in and had a nigga weak in the knees. Kima and I had been kicking for a few months, and so far, I could see myself with her, which is rare in my case because you know a nigga thinks he's Hugh Hefner. I felt myself on the verge of nutting and Kima wouldn't ease up. She just kept applying pressure.

"SHIT!" I yelled out as I came all in Kima's mouth. Kima looked up at me with them seductive brown eyes she had and a small grin formed on her face.

"You make sure you have a good day," she whispered.

I was still leaning back on the wall trying to get my shit together as Kima walked off like she just ain't win the dick sucking Olympics. Shaking my head, I adjusted my pants and flew out the door before I followed Kima and dug in her guts.

Hitting the locks on my Chevy Camaro, I hopped in and headed towards the funeral home. A nigga was grinning the entire drive. I had met Kima one night while Fiyah, Nash, and I had gone out.

Kima, of course, was Nash's sister. When I first laid eyes on her, she instantly pulled me in. The way she rocked that blonde hair and how it matched her skin so perfectly, made a nigga weak. She was a light caramel complexion, and her body was stacked. We hit it off and had been messing around ever since.

Pulling up at the funeral home, I parked my car and made my way inside. I nodded my head at the receptionist and headed on back to Fiyah's office. His door was wide open as he sat at his desk, scrolling on his phone.

"What up, nigga?" I said, dapping him up.

"Man, not shit. What took you so long to get here?" he asked, placing his phone on the desk. I grinned thinking back to Kima.

"Kima had a nigga hemmed up by the balls, literally," I said. Fiyah shook his head.

"Look at AB, you been spending a lot of time with shorty. Nash is gone fuck you up for smashing his sister. You finna throw in your playa card?" Fiyah said, pushing a plate towards me.

I grabbed the plate, and I knew it was some of Desire's cooking. She stayed looking out for a nigga.

"Normally I wouldn't even smash one of the homies family members, but it's something about shorty. I'm afraid a nigga just might be settling down. I got to know if she that one though. You know, how you got Desire's crazy ass. I need to know if Kima can hold me down the same way," I admitted.

"Kima's legit. I'm sure with a brother like Nash, he done taught her well. Plus, Desire's boughetto ass don't fuck with fake ass females," Fiyah joked but was telling the truth.

CHAPTER 5
Nash

I ain't want to dip out on shorty at all last night, but I had to stick to my word. A nigga had no intentions of starting something, and I barely knew her. Hell, it was my birthday, I needed to get my dick wet, and that was it. While driving my mind went back to last night, and the more I thought about it, a nigga was slick chasing her ass. She wasn't like the usual bitch I fucked with. My dick rocked up just thinking about how tight her shit was. All I could do was shake my head because half of me wanted to double back, and the other half wouldn't allow it.

Pulling up at my sister's place, I was going to see if I could pick her brain for a little bit about Niara. I was tripping already. I laughed at myself. Using my key, I fumbled with the lock until the door came flying open.

"The fuck you doing, Nash?" she sassed with an attitude.

"Well good morning to you too, baby sister. Who the fuck you thought I was?" I spat, pushing beside her and headed straight towards the kitchen. A nigga was dehydrated as hell.

"Why you always barging up in here like this your shit? Damn, I could've been expecting company."

"Try again, but since you been kicking it with that nigga AB. You can tell that nigga to cover some of the bills that I been paying. I ain't paying shit where another able body man is laying his head. You're out here messing with the homie like I wouldn't find out!" I snapped.

I knew something was going on between the two, but I could also tell that he really like my sister. I provided for her, so hell, if he was dicking her down, then he needed to step up to the plate as well.

"AB's got his own shit. I don't need him to pay for anything here." Kima rolled her eyes.

"Is he fucking you here on the regular?" I asked. Kima sucked her teeth and didn't say shit.

"Exactly, I'm just saying he could help. Fuck all that other rah-rah shit you talking about," I mumbled.

"You all up in my business, but where the fuck you coming from with last night's shit still on like you doing the walk of shame?" She laughed. While Kima was over there laughing if I had told her that I had fucked her friend she wouldn't be.

"Nah, ain't no walk of shame, shorty. I was slanging this thang off in something strange," I joked, and Kima and I both busted out laughing.

"Aye tho, I know I forgot to speak on it last night because a nigga was bent, but congrats on finishing up your program. You ready to open your salon?" I asked.

The one thing I promised her was when she completed school was how I would give her the funds to open her salon.

"Thanks, bro and yeah Niara and I already got everything mapped out down to the building we want."

"You know shorty well like that? You know people change once money is involved," I asked, trying to fish around.

"One you should know I don't fuck with females besides Desire, but Niara, she's a different breed. She's got her head on straight, and she got her own money, so we going half on things. She's a cool girl with a little ratchet hidden down in her. That's why I want you to stay away from her," Kima said, lifting her brow.

"I'm saying though a nigga like me eventually might settle down, so I have to test the waters."

"No sir, test that shit with someone else and leave my friend alone," Kima said in a serious tone.

"Too late." I chuckled. Kima eyes widened, and I swear her nostrils flared.

"What do you mean too late, Nashville Palero? Please don't tell me you fucked that girl?"

"Well, I won't." I shrugged. Kima grabbed the closest thing to her and threw that shit at me. I ducked dodging the paper towel holder.

"Dammit Nash, she was a virgin. Why you finna toy with that girl like that knowing you ain't shit?" she yelled.

"Man, I told her nothing was finna come from it, and I asked her if that was what she wanted to do. She was down with it, so hell, I gave her that stroke and hit the door."

"You did not tell that girl that. I swear you ain't shit, Nash. Get out! I'm so mad at you right now I'm liable to go in your shit. When I told her to get some dick, I sho as hell wasn't talking about your dog ass."

"Ouch, that hurt, sis. I love you tho but watch who the fuck you talking to," I bent down, kissed her on the cheek, and left out.

Kima

Here I was pissed at him for fucking Niara, and the whole time he knew I was fucking AB. What I was doing was different though. AB and I weren't playing with each other. Niara had me fucked up too, with her hot pussy ass.

After Nash had left, I had showered and got dressed for the day, Niara, Desire, and I was meeting up for drinks later because Desire was assisting us with the building we were looking at. I slick wanted to talk to Niara beforehand so that Desire wouldn't know her business. I wasn't mad at her, but I was trying to protect her because I knew exactly how my brother was.

I FaceTime Niara while walking to the car. When she answered the phone, she was smiling and carrying on.

"Hey, boo!" Niara's sang. I gave her a look like *you know your ass is in trouble.*

"What did you do after the club last night, or better yet who?" I asked. Niara looked around, and I hit the screen.

"Aht aht, I'm right here. I know you fucked my brother. His ass can't hold water. I tried to warn you Niara because you're my friend, so I'm saying this to say, I don't want no parts in y'all mess because I know it's about to be some."

"Kima, thank you for being concerned, but I got this boo. I'm grown, not dumb. I knew what it was once I allowed him to go any further. The dick was good, but I'm not finna chase him."

"Ewww hell no, I don't want to hear that shit. Anyway, I was just calling to tell you that. I'm about to go to Kinko's and run off these plans for later. I'll see you in a few hours," I told her and hung up the phone fast as hell.

CHAPTER 6
Niara

Maybe I was wrong, but even after Nash said what he said and we fucked twice last night afterwards, he held me. He was giving mixed signals like a motherfucker. When I woke up, and he was gone, I didn't know what to think. That second round, I initiated that shit because just that quick, I was feening, and I wanted more. I wasn't about to say shit to Kima either because I figured Nash wouldn't kiss and tell, but he fooled me.

After getting off the phone with Kima, I made my way over to my uncle's studio so that I can pick up the money that he was giving me. My uncle opened a studio in the neighborhood he grew up in to give the younger guys a reason to stay off the streets. Today the sun was shining, and I was in a good mood. Nothing could fuck up this high I was on.

Pulling into the parking lot, I pulled up beside my uncle's truck and got out. Walking inside, I headed straight to his office. All eyes were on me, and I just strutted my ass to my destination.

"Unk!" I called out when I entered. The smile that graced his face when he saw me made me happy.

"Sup baby girl? The only time you swing through is when you about to hurt my pockets." He laughed, hugging me.

"Don't do that because I know that's a lie."

"You know I'm fucking with you. You came just in time though because I was about to head out. I got an important meeting, but I wanted to make sure that I took care of you first. I'm very proud of you. You don't ask for much, so if it's anything that you need, hell if that ain't enough, I got you," he said.

"Thank you. I'm just glad school is over, and now I can work on being like you, well the boss part," I laughed. Unk chuckled and kissed me on my forehead.

"You got that right." I followed Unk out his office, and the sudden urge to pee hit me.

"You go ahead Unk I'm going to use the bathroom before I leave," I called out to him.

Running my hands through my hair, I turned around and headed down the long hall. The bathroom was on the other end and in between was different studios that folks rented out. I walked in the bathroom and was relieved to release myself even though my twat was sore as hell from last night. Finishing up, I washed my hands and then fixed the wandering strands of hair on my head. Today I was comfortable as hell rocking a wife beater, cut up jeans, and some Pumas.

Walking out of the bathroom, I made my way back down the hall this time looking through the clear glass windows at the people inside. When I got to the second set of windows, I felt my heart about to beat out my chest. It was as if Nash felt me looking at him because he turned around. I fixed my face fast as hell. I didn't know whether to wave or flick him off. The girl that was sitting in his lap turned to see what he was looking at. He stood up, shoving the girl out of his lap, making her damn near hit the floor. I was cracking up inside because he was feeling me, I could tell by his actions. As he made his way outside, I flashed a smile.

The door to the studio opened, and there Nash stood fine as ever. Crossing his arms across his chest, he looked at me up and down.

"You didn't have to come out here," I said, breaking the silence.

"Shit, you were looking like you wanted something. What

you doing over here shorty, the dick made you put a tracker on my phone?" He laughed. This cocky ass nigga, he wanted to play these games, ok.

"Please, I don't want anything in that room. Plus, I was here just picking up some money from one of my little dudes." I shrugged lying like a motherfucker. The way his jaw twitched when I said that had me laughing on the inside.

"Damn, I ain't think you were the type?" he spat. I walked closer to him because someone was walking down the hall and I was in the way.

"Look, Nash. I don't know what type of hoes you're used to dealing with," I pointed my head to ole gal that was gawking out the window like a hawk. "But, I'm the type that doesn't have to come up off no pussy just to get money. You ain't the only nigga that's barking up this tree. You sound a little salty, baby," I said with a hint of sarcasm while rubbing my hand down the side of his face.

He was pissed. Nash grabbed my hand and pulled me into the next room, which was empty. Closing the door, he locked it behind him.

"Why you playing with me, NiNi?" he hissed. I leaned back, shocked at his words.

"Oh we using nicknames now, how am I playing with you?" I laughed.

"That slick shit you popping. Any nigga that's barking up that tree needs to climb the fuck back down. I ain't having that shit," he gritted, pushing me back on the wall and pushing his tongue in my mouth. I felt like putty in his hands and kissed him back. Then I had to stand my ground, pushing him off me.

"You said you were single, right? Nothing was coming from what happened last night. Why the change of heart?" I quizzed.

Nash stood back, and he undid his pants, dropping them. His dick was poking through his boxers. My mouth started salivating at the site.

"Look what you do to me. You must be smoking dope if you thought I was about to let this pussy go." He licked his lips and grabbed my pussy.

God forgive me, I dropped to my knees and tore down his boxers, taking all of him in my mouth. A bitch could suck a mean dick, so I went to work.

"Damn, I thought you said you were a virgin?" he managed to get out in between moans.

"I never said my mouth was," I mumbled and continued to milk him. I could feel the veins pulsating, and his shit getting even harder. Then I stopped, wiped my mouth, and stood up.

"Yo, what the fuck you doing? A nigga was about to nut," he whined. Heading towards the door, I stopped and giggled.

"You remember last night before you fucked me, you said nothing would come from it? Well, nothing will come from that until you cut yo hoes off. Don't fuck with me, Nash. This ain't no regular tree. You know how to find me when you are done playing," I said in a serious tone and walked out, leaving him standing there harder than Chinese arithmetic.

I was really feeling Nash, and he needed to be honest with himself regarding me because I was not fucking sharing his ass with nobody. His little chick was standing in the hallway, and I hit her ass with a smile and blew her a kiss.

CHAPTER 7
Desire

After dropping the kids off, I still ended up being late to the funeral home. I had the mothering thing pretty much down pack, but it was a lot. Not to mention, I worked even though Fiyah was dead set on me sitting home, but I hated sitting around the house. I sat inside my car in the parking lot of the funeral home and had been sitting here for the longest watching Strokez. He was leaned against his truck engaged in a phone conversation, and he had no clue I was staring at him. Plus, my tints were so dark you couldn't even see inside my car. Strokez was a fine nigga. I ain't got no lie to tell. I didn't know too much about him except he had been working for Fiyah and AB the last year, and he was serious about his job and money. He mostly dealt with the underground work with guns and drugs.

Strokez was brown skin and had the thickest eyebrows that accented his round eyes. He rocked dreads, and that shit was long as hell. He always wore his hair in a messy bun on top of his head, and his beard always was trimmed and looking nice.

My phone buzzed, causing me to break my trance I was having. Looking down, it was a text from Fiyah asking me where the hell I was at. I rolled my eyes and placed my phone in my bag. Opening the door, I stepped out of the car, running my hands down the front of my skirt I had on. Closing the door, I locked the doors and made my way towards the funeral home. I glanced over at Strokez, who had his eyes dead on me. I nodded my head, and he threw up his hands in a peace sign. He was cheesing so hard that I could see the sparkles from his grill. I hurried and looked away, walking into the funeral home. This man was making me have thoughts that I shouldn't be having because I would never step out on my man.

"Good morning, Mrs. Cole," our new receptionist Lametrica spoke.

I greeted her with a half smile. It was something about that girl that rubbed me the wrong way. It had been a lot of changes around here, and with the opening of more funeral homes, we had to hire help. The thing is we never just hired anybody. Lametrica came when Strokez came. They were cousins. For the most part, she did her job and did it good, but I didn't trust these hoes.

I walked back to my office and threw my shit on the desk. Walking across the hall, I opened the door to Fiyah office and walked in.

"Damn, you ever heard of knocking?" Fiyah said. I looked behind me and over both shoulders to see who the fuck he was talking to.

"I don't knock on shit, just like you don't knock on shit," I told him.

"Thanks for the breakfast, Desire," AB said.

"You're welcome, nigga, now why are you blowing up my phone?" I asked Fiyah, sitting on the edge of his desk.

"Because you were tripping this morning and still ain't get here on time," he said. I couldn't do anything but laugh. Fiyah was spoiled as hell.

"Oh, you mad because I wouldn't give you no pussy?" I asked.

"Welp that's my sign to bounce, aye Desire, I do need you to do me a favor, please?" AB said, standing up.

I smacked my thigh.

"Dammit AB, what now? I'm already feeding your black ass every day?" I yelled. AB and I played around like that all the time.

"If you help a nigga out, you won't have to cook for me. Peep it. I've been seeing this chick for a few months, and I'm really feeling her, like turning in my playa card feeling her. But, I need to know if she's the one, you know if she's loyal and all that other shit like you," he said.

"AB, I'm a rare breed. Nobody is like me, but I know you've been sniffing up Kima's ass." I laughed.

"Damn, is it that noticeable?" he asked. I got quiet for a minute.

"AB's in love with Kima," Fiyah sang.

"Man, fuck you. Desire, just think about it," he said. I hopped off the desk and leaned over to kiss Fiyah.

"I'll let y'all boys handle business, and I got you AB. She's cool people," I told him.

Strokez stood by the door, and he moved out of the way as I made my way towards him. I looked down at the floor, avoiding eye contact. Jesus, his cologne smelled so good. I flew into my office and closed the door. That man had me all flustered.

I pulled out my calendar, looking over appointments that I had today. On top of that, I was meeting with Kima and Niara for drinks to discuss their upcoming business venture. I was a woman about my money and business. I refused to ever go back to the days where mama had me selling pussy. Starting on my workload, I cleared my head of my thoughts and got busy.

CHAPTER 8
Lametrica

I loved my job and the reason why because I loved the fact that I was in the presence of the Fiyah Cole. Now, I didn't come to work with intentions to woo this man, but shit, maybe one day he would look at me the way that he looked at Desire. I knew Desire didn't care too much for me. She tolerated me, but that was it. I could care less because I was after her man anyway and not her. I sat there and thought about how far I came. It was so hard for me to find a decent job that paid something due to my record I had. That's a part of growth though. When I was a teen, I was running the streets and running behind niggas that meant me no good.

The sound of laughter coming from behind me caused me to look up from the computer. It was Fiyah and AB. I swear this man was fine. I didn't want him to think I was eye-fucking him, so I turned back towards the computer and finished putting the finishing touches on the obituary that I was working on.

"Wassup Lametrica, you good up here?" Fiyah asked, his voice along made me weak.

"I'm always good," I told him acting as if he didn't have the seat of my panties wet.

I pulled my hair behind my ears and stood up at my desk. Adjusting my skirt, I knew it was hugging my ass and hips tightly. I scooped up the papers from my desk about to head to the copy room.

"Anything else?" I asked since he and AB were hawking me down.

They both shook their head, looking dumbfounded. I strutted off knowing that they were taking in my ass. I would eventually have Fiyah wrapped around my fingers. He could only resist me for so long.

I stood at the copier deep in thought watching the obits print out, and I felt a presence behind me. Turning around, I locked eyes with a smug face Desire. I smiled at her and turned back around.

"Lametrica, are you about finished with those because the family will be arriving at the church soon? Those were supposed to be printed out last night," she said with a hint of attitude.

Jesus be a fence and hold my tongue. I turned around and faced her.

"They weren't done last night, and I didn't get the finished product until this morning. I was told to hold off. Just doing what I was told," I replied as nice as I could.

"Who gave you those orders?" she questioned.

If I didn't know any better, I would say she was trying to start some shit. Fiyah entered the room, looking back and forth between Desire and me, and maybe he felt the hostility.

"What's going on?" he asked. Desire rolled her eyes at me, causing me to laugh. This girl didn't put any fear in my heart.

"She's just now printing off the obituaries for this morning's service, and the family is set to arrive soon," she told Fiyah. I was waiting on her to get here face broke.

"I told her to hold off on that until this morning because I had to add something that was last minute to it. She's good, what's the big deal?" he asked. I turned back around, grabbed the papers off the machine, and shoved them to Desire.

"All set," I said and walked out of the room heading back to my desk. I pretended as if she really pissed me off because I knew she was fucking with me on purpose, so now I was dead set on making her life a living hell.

I looked on as the two of them went back and forth about something, and then Desire stormed out of the funeral home. Fiyah was making his way towards me, and I never took my eyes off him. The way that he wore his black button-up made my mouth water. He had the sleeves rolled up, showcasing his tattoos.

"Sorry about that." He laughed. I shrugged my shoulders.

"It's ok, ever since I started working here I notice how Desire gives me a hard time. It's no biggie," I lied. Fiyah licked his lip, and when he laughed, his eyes closed shut a little making him look Chinese.

"Desire doesn't like any female that gets around me. I'll try to talk to her, but in the meantime, I again apologize for all that," he replied.

"Just buy me a drink next time we out, and I'll forget about it," I said, seeing that he always was out with my cousin Strokez when we linked. I could tell he was hesitant with his answer.

"That's cool," was all he said.

Underneath my desk, Fiyah just didn't know I was kicking my feet with joy. I just hoped that Desire stayed her mood killer ass at home.

Fiyah

When Lametrica walked off and went to the copying room. AB nor I could keep our eyes off her backside. Now, I was a faithful nigga, but I still had eyes. It was ok to look, but I had no intentions on disrespecting my woman, no matter how fine Lametrica was. I kept that shit to myself though. I ain't even tell AB that.

Lametrica was beautiful, and she caught my eye from time to time. Lametrica was about 5'2, so the little weight that she had on her made her stacked in the right places. Her caramel skin looked heavenly and soft, but I would never find out.

I stood there and watched Desire walk into the room, and I

shook my head. Desire ain't like nobody, and she had already fixed her mouth to say she didn't care for Lametrica. When I walked into the room, I knew something was off I felt it. Desire was trying to start some shit with Lametrica about her work. The way Lametrica stood there unbothered I knew it would send Desire over the edge, so I had to intervene and let her know what was up. Desire wasn't trying to hear shit I said, but I had to let her know that what she was doing was unprofessional and that was not how I ran a business. I didn't have time for no drama, or somebody getting mad and trying to sue my ass. So that's why I agreed to the drink in order to smooth things over.

CHAPTER 9
Nash

From the time that Niara left my ass there on brick and full of nut, my fucking head had been gone. That shit she pulled was foul, but I respected that shit. Shorty just don't know she was mine. I slick did want to know who the fuck she came up there for though, if I had to do a motherfucking PSA up in that bitch about her then I would.

Fiyah, AB, and I pulled up to Day Libations, and I couldn't wait to see Niara, a little birdie told me she was coming with Kima. We had the blunt going in rotation and vibing to the music. The one thing I could say we all had in common was we be stuck and in deep thought when we smoked that good shit. Pulling up beside us, Strokez hopped out the car with some little baddie. She walked on in the building, and Strokez hopped in the whip with us joining the smoke session.

"Aye, I ain't tell y'all this shit when it happened, but the other day, I was in the basement taking care of some business and when I got to looking at dude before I pushed him in the retort, guess who the fuck it was?" Fiyah said as he blew out the smoke. Reaching for the blunt, I looked at him.

"Who nigga? You have been secretive as hell lately with that burning motherfuckers up and shit," I asked.

"Agatha son," Fiyah laughed. If you were close to Fiyah, then you knew who Agatha was. AB and I busted out laughing.

"Man two braids?" I joked. Fiyah looked at me crazy with low eyes. Strokez busted out laughing in the back seat.

"Fuck you, Nash. You always got some jokes funny looking ass nigga. Man, I beat the shit out of him on that table and damn near forgot he was already dead," Fiyah grinned. The nigga was over there dealing with something in his head, and I wasn't about to go any further into that situation.

"Man, fuck all that. I'm ready to grab me a bitch. Let's go," Strokez called out, stepping out of the car. I finished off the blunt and hopped out the car.

"You tell Desire you were coming out?" I asked Fiyah. He screwed his face up.

"Nigga, I don't have to check in with her. I'm just coming to have a drink that's it. She's probably still pissed off about me shutting her down earlier from trying to start shit with Lametrica!" he spat.

"Who the hell is that?" I asked.

"Shorty that got out the car with Strokez, his cousin," AB jumped in.

"Aw hell, yeah, she's going to be mad for a while," I told him.

We walked in, and Strokez was chilling in the cabana with Kima and Niara. Niara was looking edible as hell. I walked towards her licking my lips like she was the last piece of spicy Popeyes chicken in the box. She had this sneaky smirk on her face probably wondering why I was there. I winked at Kima, who rolled her eyes.

"Why you keep looking at me like that?" she blushed.

"Because you're beautiful," I whispered. Her mouth dropped, and I shook my head at myself. She got me sounding sappy as fuck.

"I assume you ready to stop playing?" she asked.

"I'm here, ain't I?" was all I said.

Strokez

"What you over there thinking?" my cousin Lametrica leaned towards me and asked.

"Not shit, that Xan I took is kicking in, plus we smoked in the car, so I'm feeling good than a motherfucker," I replied.

"Give me one?" Lametrica asked.

I reached into my pockets and pulled the baggie out. While under the table, I removed two pills and handed them to her. I watched as she threw one back and took a sip of her drink.

"What the fuck y'all over there taking?" Fiyah asked.

I peeped how Lametrica smelled this nigga hair when he leaned in front of her to talk to me. I couldn't do shit but shake my head. She was playing a dangerous game.

"Xannies, my nigga," I told him.

"You want one. I have an extra one?" Lametrica asked him. I tuned out their conversation and started focusing on the shorty that was across the way. I signaled for the waitress to come here.

"Can I help you?" she asked.

"Can you go over to that table and whatever the girl in the pink shirt is drinking, get her another one," I told her.

When she walked off, I kept my gaze on shorty. I watched as the waitress walked over to her table. Shorty looked at me, and I hit her with a head nod. She looked a little stuck-uppish, but she shocked my ass as she was making her way over to me.

"You want to buy me a drink?" she asked.

"I was trying to, is that a problem?"

"No, I liked what I saw, so I decided to come over." She smiled, showing this chipped ass tooth she had. Fuck, shorty was bad though. I hope this tooth don't be a distraction.

Niara

I could've sworn that this was supposed to be a business

meeting, and when I looked up, the whole damn gang was here. Seeing Nash, I just knew his ass was about to be pissed about that shit I pulled, but it worked out. Everyone was vibing, and you would've thought we were all couples. I had just met Desire last night, but the shit I was seeing I was hoping that I wasn't overacting. She hadn't got here yet, but this other chick that was supposed to be Strokez cousin was a little too chummy with Fiyah. I hated to bust up Kima groove with AB, but I nudged her in her arm. Kima leaned over to me.

"Let me know if I'm overacting, but where the fuck is Desire and why the hell is that chick all in her husband's face?" I whispered.

Kima sucked her teeth.

"You ain't tripping but trust and believe I already told her to get here stat," she mouthed and turned back to AB.

"You all worried about the next nigga when you need to be entertaining me, ma," Nash raspy voice vibrated my ear.

I picked up the glass of water that was sitting in front of me and took a sip. After all that drinking from last night, I wasn't about to drink anything else.

"One thing you will see about me is I'm huge on loyalty. I can tell now that you guys' circle is close knit, and that shit ain't cool. I would hope you spoke some sense into your boy."

"That shit ain't got nothing to do with me. For one, you females look into stuff way more than it seems. The shit looks innocent to me." Nash shrugged.

Shaking my head, I wasn't buying that bullshit, and I hoped like hell Desire walked into the door now rather than later.

CHAPTER 10
Lametrica

When Fiyah leaned in front of me, the scent of his Gucci Guilty, hit me like a ton of bricks. His freshly braided hair was braided straight back, and his goatee freshly cut. This nigga was everything. After about fifteen minutes, my bar had started to kick in, and I was feeling the music. The drinks were coming, and everyone was having a good time. Strokez was booed up with some chick that I didn't know, Nash and this other chick kept eyeballing the fuck out of me, and AB and Kima were in they own world. That left Fiyah and I looking like outsiders.

I stood up because I had to go to the bathroom and immediately got dizzy falling into Fiyah's lap.

"Whoa, you good?" he asked. AB and Kima looked up with confused looks on their faces.

"Yes, I guess I got up to fast. I'm heading to the bathroom." I laughed.

I was fucked up for real. I managed to get by, and I headed straight to the bathroom. When I got in the bathroom, I locked the door behind me and stared in the mirror at myself. My eyes were low as hell. I smiled at myself and proceeded to use the bathroom. Once I finished, I washed my hands and unlocked the door. Pushing the door open, when I exited, I walked dead smack into Fiyah.

"Ouch, shit. Excuse me!" I yelled. Fiyah had his hands on my arms, keeping me from falling.

"It's aite. I shouldn't have been standing so close to the door. I was just trying to see if you made it to the bathroom, and if you were ok," he said.

I fixed my clothes and held my gaze with him. I didn't know if I was making him uncomfortable or not, but I wanted to suck his lips off his face. Maybe he sensed it because he licked his lips, and I noticed he shook his head in a no motion.

"You good?" I asked.

"Yeah, I'm straight. Where you park, I need to sit down away from all this noise," he asked.

I led us out of the exit door and into the parking lot to my car. I was fumbling with the keys trying to get the door unlocked when I dropped the keys.

"Let me help you," Fiyah said he bent down to get my keys but placed them in his pocket, instantly catching me off guard.

"What are you doing?" I asked.

"Sssh," he slurred in my ear.

Fiyah pressed his body against mine and had me up against the car. His hands started to roam my body until he had my pants halfway down in the back. Within seconds, I felt him slide inside of me. A small gasp escaped my lips, as Fiyah continued to hit me with fast strokes. I couldn't get out a word. This wasn't how I envisioned my first time with him to be. I was so excited though that I was super wet. I looked back over my shoulder at Fiyah, who was still shaking his head.

"Man, this shit ain't right, my girl gone kill me," he moaned, but he kept stroking.

I was going to get mine. I didn't care about no damn guilt trips he was having. Hell, it couldn't have been that damn bad because he was still knee-deep in my pussy. Here we were outside like a motherfucker, and I was praying that we didn't get caught.

"Man, damn!" Fiyah yelled as he tightened his grip around my waist. He pulled out and stepped back, trying to adjust his pants.

I held my hand out, motioning for my keys. After he placed them in my hands, I unlocked the door and popped the truck grabbing some wipes from my overnight bag that I kept in my car when I stayed with Strokez some nights.

"If you want to clean yourself up, I got some wipes here," I told him. I grabbed a few and cleaned off, disposing them in the bushes nearby. This was some real hoe shit. Pulling my pants up, I leaned up against the car with my arms crossed. Once Fiyah took care of his hygiene, he had a look of shame on his face.

"Lametrica, you a real dope girl, but that wasn't supposed to happen. I let the drinks and the way that pill had me feeling take over. If I led you on in any way, I'm sorry. Are you on any kind of birth control?" he asked.

Shaking my head no, he let out a huge sigh. I watched as he reached into his pocket and handed me some money.

"Can you please get a Plan B? I can't have no shit coming back on a nigga," he said.

That was one thing about me. I was one that could control my emotions because I knew he was under the influence. That was the plan. Even though I didn't expect things to happen the way they did, I was going to still show him that I was the one he needed on his team. I grabbed the money from him.

"Let me go back in first so that it won't look suspicious," he said. Fiyah headed back into Day Libations, and I stood there laughing.

CHAPTER 11
Desire

One thing about it, I was going to always pop up on the scene when it came to mine. All it took was for Kima to tell me to get to Day Libations and fast because my man was there not alone. Yeah, I was still a little salty from earlier with the shit that went down with Fiyah and that whore Lametrica. I had every right to be. I felt she was trying to push up on my man, and I was never wrong about my intuitions. When I walked in Kima signaled me over to the cabana where they were seated.

Right off the bat, my antennas went up because Fiyah and Lametrica were missing. Kima and AB were booed up, Niara and Nash were vibing, and even Strokez's fine chocolate ass was entertaining some bitch.

"Wassup y'all!" I greeted everyone. Nash looked like a deer caught in headlights.

"Damn Desire, where you come from?" he had the nerve to ask.

"I'm always around, where's my man at?" I asked, getting straight to the point. Nash didn't have an answer.

"I think he said he had to use the bathroom," Strokez quickly said.

"Wassup, baby?" I heard Fiyah's voice when I turned around he was making his way through the front entrance.

"Where you coming from?" I asked.

"I had gone to the bathroom," he said, taking a seat beside

Strokez.

"So, the bathroom is outside? Why you coming in the front door?" I spat. He was about to make me go in his shit.

"Man, get a nigga another drink, the same thing I had," Fiyah told the waitress. I stood there with my arms crossed.

"Come on, sis, sit down. We in a different establishment and y'all can save that shit for when you get home," AB said.

I took my seat beside Fiyah even though I was boiling on the inside. Kima handed me a drink, and I started drinking on the fruity mix. Not even five minutes later there she was. She strolled in flipping her hair over her shoulders. I ain't gone lie. When Lametrica wasn't dressed in work clothes, her body was banging. Her jeans looked as if they were painted on they hugged her curves perfectly. The way her breasts sat up perfectly in her shirt, this whore's body was sickening in the nicest way. I watched as she took a seat beside Strokez, and they exchanged words.

"Where you coming from?" I asked. She leaned forward and looked at me like she was crazy.

"Excuse me?" she asked.

"You come marching in here right after my man, I just find it funny," I said. It was no point in lying.

"You don't wear that look well. What is it with you and this thing you got going about Fiyah and me?" she asked.

"You just seem sneaky as hell, like a snake with a motive. Admit it you attracted to him?" I snapped. Fiyah and everyone started laughing.

"This is stupid. Can I get some water? I sort of got something thick caught in my throat," she said, winking at Fiyah. That was it, I tried to hop over the table and snatch this hoe. Strokez grabbed her and carried her outside, and I looked at Fiyah.

"What the fuck is she talking about?" I hissed.

"You are tripping Desire forreal. Ain't nothing happened

between her and me," he said, but I felt he was lying.

"Let's go. I'm ready to go home," I told him.

"Bruh, please take her ass the fuck on before she starts pistol popping in this bitch," AB sighed.

Fiyah jerked me up with the quickness. Once outside, I pulled away from him.

"I swear Desire, you on some stupid shit right now!" he yelled. We hopped in the car, and I just sat there and looked at him. This man must have forgotten that I knew him like the back of my hand.

"Would you start the fucking car?" he yelled.

"I'll start the fucking car when I get ready. I thought we were better than that Fiyah. Everything that we done been through we have never lied to each other, so why start now?" I yelled.

I loved him more than anything, and he had never cheated on me. I just wanted him to tell me the truth. I smelled her perfume on him. Fiyah ran his hands over his face like he was frustrated.

"Did you fuck her, or did she suck your dick?" I just came out and asked.

"Man, nall she ain't suck my dick," he said.

"So, you fucked her?" I replied quickly. Fiyah whole chest did this fall like he felt defeated.

"The shit didn't even last ten minutes," he whispered.

WOP! WOP!

I hauled off and started throwing punches.

"So, this whole time, when y'all came back in at different times. You had been fucking her. I knew it!" I hit the steering wheel.

"That shit wasn't supposed to happen. We both were on them bars, and I made the first move so don't think that girl was making passes and shit. I took her keys and initiated everything right there outside," he said. *Outside.*

"Really outside? She is fired," I blurted out.

"How are you going to fire her when it wasn't her fault? That shit was on me," he had the nerve to say.

"Do you not hear yourself? How do you expect me to work in the same building as her knowing she done fucked my husband? You're a married man, Fiyah Cole, or did you forget?" I spat.

"Ain't nobody forget," he whispered.

My head was killing me, and I knew my pressure was up. Starting the car, I pulled out in traffic and headed home.

"You fire her, or I will, and if I do it, it won't be good?" I told him.

"You're not thinking, Desire. This could start some shit, and she might try to take a nigga down with a sexual harassment suit. Anything can happen," he said. I kept my eyes on the road.

"That's not my problem, and I don't care. You should've thought about that before you stuck your dick all up in there for ten minutes," I told him.

The only thing I was focused on right now was Ashlyn and Ashton. Fiyah had me so pissed was he gone make me kick his ass.

CHAPTER 12
Fiyah

A nigga felt bad as hell for even having to lie to Desire. She didn't deserve that at all. As she said, she knew me better than I knew my damn self. She was going to pry that shit out of me anyway, so I went ahead and told her the truth. Desire ass was crazy, so I had to work something out with Lametrica because I didn't want to fire her from her job. I laid my head back on the seat and just stared at the ceiling the whole drive home. I was done talking, and I knew Desire was over there having a field day in her head.

I closed my eyes, and images of Lametrica were popping up in my head, and I couldn't figure out why. I didn't even see that girl in that type of way, but I ain't gone lie. That pussy was good.

The car jerked, and I opened my eyes, realizing that we were home.

Desire hopped out the car slamming the door, and I sat there for a minute before getting out. I pulled the blunt I had tucked behind my ear out and lit it up. Taking a long pull, I let the smoke fill my lungs and elevate me. I just knew I wasn't going to be able to go in here and go to bed. For some strange reason, I felt that Desire wasn't done with her mess. My phone rang, and I looked down at the screen. It was Nash calling.

"What nigga?" I answered.

"Nigga, I was just trying to see if your yella ass was still breathing. What the hell is going on?" he asked.

I wasn't about to discuss shit with him over the phone because I didn't even want to talk about it.

"Man, I'll holla at you later about all that. I'm just focused on waking up in the morning." I laughed. Nash was cracking up on the other end of the phone.

"Aite, love you fool," he said.

"Love you too, bro," I told him then ended the call.

I got out of the car and headed inside the house, which was dark as hell. Walking upstairs, I dragged my ass to the bedroom. Reaching for the doorknob, that shit wouldn't turn. I closed my eyes because I just knew Desire was on some petty shit.

"Desire, if you don't unlock this fucking door, you already know what the fuck is going to happen!" I yelled.

"Go sleep your ass in the other room, cheating ass!" she yelled back.

"I wish the fuck you would try and tell me where to go sleep in my own house. Open this door!" I spat and kicked the door.

There was some slight movement, and then I saw the lights cut off. I scooted back away from the door, and she had better hope she wasn't on the other side because I was about to kick this bitch in. I ran towards the door and kicked the door with all my might.

"You bout a stupid motherfucker," Desire hissed.

I ignored her ass and walked straight to the bathroom so that I could shower before getting in bed. I could care less about her tantrum. Once in the shower, I took my time soaping up my body and letting the water just run over me. Once the water started getting cold, I turned it off and stepped out. Grabbing my durag, I tied my hair down and brushed my teeth.

When I walked back in the bedroom, Desire was sitting up in the bed reading. We locked eyes, and the way she looked at me slick broke a nigga's heart because we didn't have moments like this. I dropped the towel and put me a pair of Polo underwear on.

One thing I couldn't do was go to bed without telling Desire I loved her and that I was sorry. Even though she was mad, that wasn't us. I slid in the bed under the covers and turned to Desire. She didn't even bother looking my way.

"We have never gone to bed like this before, and again, I want to say that I'm sorry. I love you Desire Cole, and I know it may take some time for you to forgive me, but I promise you I will never do no shit like that again," I told her, meaning every word.

Desire continued to read and didn't respond. Letting out a huge sigh because I tried, I just turned over and laid down.

"I love you too," Desire finally spoke. That's all I wanted to hear, and now I could sleep peacefully.

Niara

Baby when I say shit hit the fan, that shit hit the fan. Now, I ain't gone lie. When Desire walked in, I was like yes in my head. I had no clue that she was going to come while Fiyah and Lametrica had disappeared. Nash had to pay them people some money to keep quiet because, of course, everyone knew who the hell Fiyah and Desire was around town.

Nash had followed me home, where we showered, well fucked and then showered, and now we were sitting here in the living room with a blunt in rotation. Looking at him, I wanted to know everything about him. Nash turned to look at me catching me in gawking mode. I quickly turned my head.

"Aye tho, on some real shit, my homie said you came up there to the studio and was chopping it up with my OG. Then you holler you came and got some money. Please tell me you ain't fucking with Rodney's old ass?" Nash blew smoke out and kept his eyes on me. That's exactly what my ass gets for lying.

"Rodney is my uncle." I laughed. I could see his face relax but then tense up some more.

"You bullshitting?"

"No, I'm not. He and my mom are brother and sister. He raised me."

"Are you fucking serious? That nigga took me under his wing when I was sixteen. That nigga is the plug. I know he finna have some shit to say about this here." He chuckled.

"Well, make him not have anything to say. I assume since you sitting up here in my face you have a reputation that you claim you're gonna change. I gave you a chance to run and continue to do you. Just know I might carry myself with class but ain't no hoe in my blood and my uncle didn't raise no doormat," I flat out told him, and I was serious.

"Look, don't get me wrong. I'm used to certain shit. A nigga got mad bitches out here. Regardless of what I do, they gone flock to a nigga. That's all they know. I'm selfish with the things I want only for me. So, don't get mad when I have a hard time or forget that I'm even trying this shit for the time being. You just don't know how much I'm gone change your life, shorty. A nigga ain't never just met a bitch worth changing for."

"For the time being? You have that much doubt in yourself that you can't be with one woman? I got a feeling I'm about to be fighting a lot. Nall, look how I sound? I ain't fighting over shit but respect, and that's only if I have to. I might have to fight your ass a few times. So now you got to take me on a date," I looked at Nash to read his face because I was serious.

"Bruh, do I look like I go on dates?" He stood up.

"No date, no more cake." I shrugged and headed to the bedroom.

I could hear Nash let out a huge sigh, but he followed behind me. Climbing in bed, he walked over and laid across the bottom part of my bed. I asked no questions.

"Goodnight, Nash!" I hollered over my shoulders.

"Yeah, aite," he mumbled. He thought I was playing, but he wasn't getting any more pussy from my ass until he took me out on a date.

CHAPTER 13
AB

The ringing of my cell phone woke me up out my sleep. I slid my arm from underneath Kima and grabbed the phone off the dresser.

"Yo," I said into the phone still sounding like sleep.

"Aye, we got a drop before the funeral home open, and the bag is in your trunk, nigga," Fiyah's voice boomed through the phone. I sat up and rubbed the sleep from my eyes.

"Damn, I forgot all about that shit. Let me get dressed and drop it off," I said.

"Nah bruh, come and scoop my ass. I got to handle some shit before the doors open," he mumbled.

"Bet, give me fifteen minutes," I told him, ending the call.

Placing the phone back on the dresser, I stood up, adjusted my dick in my boxers, and did a nice little stretch. Looking back, Kima was snoring peacefully. I headed to the bathroom and took care of my hygiene. Once finished, I stepped into the closet and grabbed a sweatshirt and some joggers throwing them on. I walked over to Kima, giving her a slight shove.

"Baby, I got to go handle some shit, but I'll be back," I told her. She nodded her head and rolled right back over and closed her eyes.

Grabbing my keys, I headed to the garage. Popping the trunk, I unzipped the bag and looked at the contents making sure everything was everything. Satisfied, I closed the trunk and hopped in the car. I always kept me a blunt rolled, so I reached into the ashtray and lit that bitch up. Turning on the radio, I put on me some NBA Youngboy and backed out of the garage. Fiyah stayed about five minutes away, so hopefully, he was ready because I wasn't getting out of the car.

I pulled up in front of his crib and laid on the horn. I knew that would piss him off. That nigga opened the door fast as hell. His yella ass had a frown on his face. I hit the locks on the door, and he jerked the door open getting inside.

"Motherfucker is you crazy?" he spat. I passed him the blunt.

"Here and shut the hell up. Where am I going?" I asked before pulling off.

"I done had to call Strokez ass and try to get Lametrica address, but he said she was at his crib. I need to go over there and make shit right because Desire doesn't want her ass at the funeral home no more," he told me.

"Nigga, so you did smash? What the hell you making right? What wifey's crazy ass says goes," I told him. Fiyah shook his head.

"Normally I wouldn't care bout no bitch feelings, and even now I don't, but I just don't want to fire her because I came on to her. I don't know if that girl is struggling, or if she really needs a job. I just need to talk to her." Fiyah sighed.

"I noticed you said you initiated. So, she wasn't throwing that pussy at you?" I asked. I knew Fiyah, and he wouldn't cheat on Desire, so this shit was somewhat shocking that he was willing to risk it all.

"Man, I don't know what the hell it was. I was just trying to be helpful at first and check on her because I knew she was fucked up when she went to the bathroom. Shit, a nigga went back there, and we ended up going outside. A nigga just pushed up on her, well shit, I pulled her pants down and slid right in. The whole time I was saying this shit ain't right, but hell, I couldn't even stop," he said, shaking his head.

Now, I know we played around a lot, but I knew this was serious, and Fiyah was trying to keep things smooth and drama-free in his home.

"Did you at least strap up?" I asked. I could tell by Fiyah body language that he didn't.

"Man, I gave her some money for a plan B," he said. I just shook my head.

"I'm your boy and shit, and you know I ain't gone bite my tongue, but this is some of the stupidest shit that you done ever did, my nigga," I said, telling him the truth.

I pulled into the driveway and cut the engine.

"Let me go in here and handle this so we can drop this shit off." He sighed.

Fiyah

I couldn't even be mad at AB for telling me how he felt because I did do some stupid shit. I skipped up the steps and knocked on the door. Strokez lived in a nice little duplex on the east side.

Strokez came to the door.

"Wassup nigga?" he greeted me dapping me up. I walked inside the house, taking a look around.

"I'm gone step outside and holla at AB. Lametrica was brushing her teeth, so she should be down in a minute," he said.

I hit him with a head nod and took a seat on the couch. I grabbed the picture frame that was on the table, and it was a picture of Lametrica and Strokez when they were kids. I placed the frame back down.

"Wassup Fiyah?" her angelic voice said.

Lametrica stood there dressed in a pair of yoga pants and a crop top. She had her hair pulled up. She rocked a pair of glasses that I didn't even know she wore. She must've worn contacts when she came to work. It made her look sophisticated and smart, even with all the tattoos she had.

"Aye wassup, Lametrica? I really came over to talk to you about last night and kind of let you know where we at with everything," I started.

"Last night didn't happen, right? You don't have to tell me to keep my mouth shut," she said.

"Nah this ain't about that. My wife knows what went down, and she doesn't want you working for us anymore. Now, I don't know your situation, but I have to respect my wife wishes. What I will do is continue to pay you for a couple of months until you find something else since this was all my fault," I insisted.

Lametrica walked over to me and sat down beside me on the couch.

"It wasn't all your fault because I wanted it to happen, and I've been wanting that for a long time. I understand why you have to keep wifey happy, so it's no hard feelings," she said.

She was taking this shit better than I thought.

"Cool, well here," I said, reaching into my pocket and hit her with a nice size chunk.

"This should hold you until the end of the month. I got to go though. Be easy," I said, standing up and heading out the door. Strokez was walking back towards the house.

"Hit me when you ready for a nigga to come through," he said.

"Aite fool," I told him.

I got settled in the car and felt like I handled that situation good. Something was weighing on me though, and I couldn't place it at the moment. AB started the car, and we headed to the funeral home to make this drop.

CHAPTER 14
Desire

Last night was a painful situation no matter how hard I tried to block it out. I knew that marriages weren't perfect, but I had that ounce of hope that at least Fiyah and I was damn near. When he told me that he had slept with Lametrica, I wasn't really going to show him how hurt I was. Instead, I had to show him the anger that resonated inside. I knew he was sorry about everything based on the way he spoke before we went to bed last night. Life is extremely short, and we couldn't go to bed mad at one another. I knew he was going to handle things with Lametrica, one thing I knew he ain't want me to handle that shit.

I moved around the kitchen freely getting Ashlyn and Ashton prepared for school and daycare. Fiyah left out of here so fast, and I didn't want the kids to sense anything because I still wasn't talking to him. One thing though I wasn't going to end our marriage over this because it was only a one-time thing. The thoughts I had about Strokez were just as bad. The only thing was I didn't act on any of it, so long as he didn't know, shit then he would never know.

Once Ashlyn and Ashton finished breakfast, we got ready to head out. Fiyah knew that I was going to be late if I had to drop the kids off, and the fact that he hadn't made it back home to change was bothering me because we had a family coming this morning. Loading the kids in the car, I called Fiyah's cell, which immediately went to voicemail. I was starting to get frustrated.

Starting the car, I backed out of the driveway. While driving,

I hit the Bluetooth and decided to call AB phone in hopes that he would answer. This nigga didn't answer his phone either.

"Shit," I said.

"Ooh mama, bad word." Ashlyn giggled.

"I'm sorry sweetie," I told her looking over my shoulder. Checking the time, I had to resort to another measure, so I called Strokez. He answered on the first ring.

"What's up, Desire?" Strokez voice came through the phone. I shook my head because damn, he sounded good.

"Have you seen Fiyah or AB?" I asked.

I heard movement in the background. I pulled up into the parking spot, getting ready to walk Ashlyn in.

"I saw them this morning they said they were headed to the funeral home. They accidentally left some shit in the car," he answered.

"Nobody is answering the phone, and I still have to drop Ashton off. Can you please go over there and just make the Jackson family comfortable until I arrive, especially if they're not there?" I pleaded.

At this point, I just needed somebody there hell if he couldn't go Lametrica could even take her ass.

"Aite, I'll head on over there," he said.

"Thank you." I sighed and ended the call. I was in out of the daycare in no time and then headed straight to Ashton school to drop him off.

About thirty minutes later, I finally arrived at the funeral home only to see AB car wasn't here. My phone started ringing, and I answered the phone fast and irritated as hell.

"Hello!" I yelled into the phone.

"You have a collect call from, Fiyah," I stood there mouth wide and froze damn near dropping the phone.

Fiyah

AB was still rambling on about this cheating shit as if he been a motherfucking saint his whole life. I couldn't wait to hop out the car from this nigga. We hit the corner, and I noticed a cop car turn behind us.

"I hope you ain't flying nigga, twelve just pulled behind us," I told AB. AB looked up in the rearview and nodded his head. No soon as he did that, them blue lights came on.

"Shit, you know how this shit goes, AB. Pull over," I told him.

Yeah, we were criminals, and we did dirty shit, so we knew the game. Our asses weren't invincible, but we had the dopest lawyer on standby. One thing we did as one was take the heat so we were prepared just in case this shit went south.

AB pulled the car over, and we watched as the officer got out of the car and made his way to the vehicle.

"Morning, officer!" AB spoke. *This nigga.*

"You know your tail light is out and whatever loud you are smoking is just that loud," the officer said. AB started laughing, and I wanted to smack this nigga in the back of his head.

"I wasn't aware the tail light was out," AB replied.

"I need you to step out the car," was all he said.

I knew then this shit wasn't going to be good. AB did as he was told another car pulled up. Now you know when that second car pulled up, all hope of us going home was a done deal. The second officer walked up and asked me to step out the car, and I did. AB and I sat on the sidewalk with our hands behind our back as we watched them search the vehicle. Of course, they ain't find shit but the damn bag.

"What the hell y'all doing riding around with this much cash?" one of the officers asked.

"I own Cole Funeral Home and Crematory Services. I have all

the paperwork so that money is accounted for," I told the officer.

A nigga wasn't dumb. Now the guns were another story. The officer spoke into his walkie-talkie as if he was calling to check that shit.

"So, explain the guns. Y'all need those to run the funeral home?" he asked. Neither AB nor I spoke a word.

"Aw, so now y'all both want to get quiet?" he asked with a hint of sarcasm. There wasn't shit to say, I knew Desire was going to pitch a bitch once she got my phone call because we were going down, and she was in charge.

During the ride to the station, I just sat and thought about how I had never got caught slipping in nothing that I did, and then this shit happened. I was so mad at myself for being too fucked up last night that I couldn't do what the hell I needed to do right away. Had I been on my shit, we would have never had to make that run this morning.

As soon as I got to the station, I ran into Detective Mac. He was an old friend. He immediately went to work our case, especially trying to see what the hell they had written on the report and shit. I was given my call, and when I called Desire, my stomach was hurting like a motherfucker because I feared her reaction, but if anything, I knew she would handle things like a boss, and Strokez was there to assist.

When I heard her voice, and she accepted the call, I went into order mode running off a list of things I needed her to do with speaking as less as possible because I knew the phones were recording everything.

"I need for you to handle all affairs. Those that you don't know of just think hard on it and stroke your temple. I had an important lunch today. Man, I wanted that Manicotti and three different kinds of cheese and a Milos sweet tea. Maybe next time, I'll talk to you soon, and I love you," was all I needed to say and was going to say on the phone.

Desire knew that I spoke in code basically telling her and Strokez to handle everything, and what she didn't know Strokez was in charge. I also told her that we got caught with money and three different guns, so she needed to call my lawyer Miles and let him handle that. Hanging up the phone, I sat back in my seat and now it was the waiting game.

CHAPTER 15

Desire

I stood there in the middle of the floor of the funeral home in shock. I couldn't believe Fiyah and AB had got hemmed up. I was literally at a loss for words. Strokez walked up towards me with a concerned look on his face.

"Yo, you good?" he asked. Shaking out of my thoughts, I spoke a little bit above a whisper.

"Fiyah and AB have been arrested with money and guns. As of now, we are in charge of everything. I have to place a call to Miles, so I'm going to make this call and then get this family out of here as fast as I can. I really hate to do this because I honestly want to beat your cousin's face in, but I need you to get her on the phone and get her down here. I can't do this by myself and handle Fiyah's shit also, and I most definitely can't close down for business," I told him.

It took a lot for me to put this shit to the side for now, but trust and believe, Lametrica was going to get confronted.

"Cool, I'll call Nash so that he can call Kima about AB because she's probably clueless as hell. I apologize for my cousin, I wasn't aware of no fuck shit, and I hate that anything like that happened, but we got this," Strokez said and patted me on the shoulder before walking off.

I put on a huge smile because I had to go in here and apologize to this family for having them wait only to have to dismiss myself again to call this lawyer.

***

A few hours later, I had the family taken care of and gone. Miles had been called and was looking into the situation with Fiyah and AB. I sat here in my office slick on stuck because until I knew exactly what I was dealing with, I didn't know what to call on what. There was a knock on my office door.

"Come in!" I yelled. The door opened, and Kima came strolling in with panic etched on her face.

"What the hell is going on?" Kima asked her voice was shaky. I fixed the look on my face because I know it was looking stank.

"I thought you were Lametrica. I'm waiting to hear back from Miles, but Fiyah and AB got caught up in a situation. Everything should be good though," I said.

Saying it aloud was really me reassuring myself. Was I ready to handle everything if Fiyah had to go away for a little bit? This was about to be a lot, not to mention juggling two kids.

"I take it things didn't go so well last night with the Fiyah and Lametrica situation?" she asked. I sat back in my chair.

"No, they didn't. Fiyah fessed up. That hoe slept with my husband!" I spat. All Kima did was shake her head.

"That shit was fucked up, and she'd better keep her distance because I'm liable to smack fire from her ass," I said, telling Kima the truth.

"Niara peeped that shit. I didn't think it was going to go that far, but now we have other things to be concerned about." Kima sighed.

"You right, you right." I calmed down, massaging my temples. Kima started laughing.

"We didn't even get to do what we initially were supposed to do yesterday. Until things get situated, I'll let Niara know we got to postponed things for a bit," she said.

"One thing for sure is AB will be straight, I did have time to look over the paperwork, and things look good. Shit, if you got the deposit, I'll let my guy know that y'all ready to move forward. Always remember when dealing with these niggas to always keep yourself first," I told Kima.

"I might have to run to the Mexican spot so that I can have me a margarita or two. Niara wants to link, you want to join?" Kima asked.

"Shit, let's go," I said. I turned off the computer monitor and grabbed my bag.

We both walked out of the office and headed towards the front. When I got to the front, Lametrica was sitting there at the front desk, and Strokez stood there. They stopped talking when Kima and I entered the room.

"Heard anything?" Strokez asked.

"Not yet, and if I did, it would not be discussed in front of those that don't need to be in our business!" I spat making sure I mugged the hell out of Lametrica. This hoe started laughing. It took everything in me not to drag her from that desk and into one of these caskets in here. Sucking my teeth, I headed out the door.

***

Kima, Niara, and I were at Las Maracas having lunch and, of course, a drink because my nerves were frazzled. I have yet to receive a call about Fiyah, and I wasn't sure what the hell was going on. Niara was very supportive, and I could tell that she was loyal. I was huge on vibes, and ever since Kima introduced us, I peeped that. Kima didn't fuck with everybody, which was why we were so close.

I took a sip of the cold, frozen drink when my phone started ringing. I held my hand up to silence them.

"Hey Miles, what's up?" I asked. I was so anxious.

"Ok, so I got some mixed news. Fiyah and AB are heading to serve time right now. They both took the charges on the guns.

The money you can come pick up because it was accounted for with the business. Listen carefully though. You need to get some cash to Mac because he had the ballistics from the guns thrown out, so nothing could be added to time. Now both Fiyah and AB are looking at three to four years possible early release, so they won't have to do the whole thing," he rambled off.

My heart dropped right along with my mouth. I even felt a teardrop. Hell, I was still stuck on them doing time.

"Wait go back, why the hell are they taking these charges?" I asked.

"They're both claiming the guns. Desire, this is the best deal they could've got. Can you imagine the time they would've gotten had Mac didn't clear them ballistics? Be smart, Desire. Take care of what I told you, and I'm sure once Fiyah gets settled, he will call you," Miles said.

"Thank you, Miles," I mumbled in the phone.

Placing the phone down on the table, I looked at Kima and Niara. Swallowing the lump in my throat, before I even opened my mouth, Kima started shaking her head.

"I assume it wasn't good news?" Kima asked. I nodded my head.

"They finna have to do some time. They're looking at about three years. I swear them niggas is loyal as hell to one another. Instead of one taking the charges, they both claimed the guns. I don't know if you really feeling AB or if this is some sort of fling, but if you feel you can't handle this, then you might as well leave now because he ain't got nobody but us. That's why we all so close," I told Kima.

Kima looked as if she was caught off guard.

"You're one of them people just don't care what comes out your mouth, Desire. You fucking know me better than that, and for you to even say some shit like that, I'm going to blame the shock because you know damn well I ain't built like that. The fuck I look like bouncing. That's my brother's friend. I ain't going nowhere because I like Ahmad, I knew exactly what I was getting myself into when I started messing with him. So, there is no need for all that!" she spat.

"Ok, y'all just calm down. Y'all are both letting your emotions cloud your judgment," Niara jumped in.

"I'm just saying because three years is a long time for anyone, fuck even me. Dammit, Fiyah! I have to get this money to this detective," I said jumping up, leaving both of them sitting there.

I knew my emotions were at an all-time high at the moment, and that's why I was lashing out. How in the fuck was I supposed to tell my kids this shit? Then on top of that, I needed to boss the fuck up, which wasn't a problem because I done been down for worse. This shit was just unexpected, but I guess even the best get caught slipping. Placing my shades on my face, I walked out of the restaurant to my car.

"Bitch, boss up or go broke. Your last name ain't Cole for nothing," I said aloud.

CHAPTER 16
Niara

It had been approximately a month and seventeen days since Nash and I hooked up that night of his birthday. Things were going well, but for me, they were just a bit fast. Don't get me wrong. I was feeling him, and I could see him doing everything to stay on the right track, but unfortunately, we have hit a slight bump in the road.

My plans had been derailed, and I was adamant about getting them back on track. Looking over at Desire, she was focused on the road. I was happy that she could take the time out of her day to assist me, especially with all the changes in her life right now with Fiyah being sent to the pen. Looking back out the window, I let out a deep sigh. I prayed that God forgives me for what I was about to do. Desire pulled up and parked, cutting the car off. We both looked at each other.

"Look Niara. You don't have to do this shit. Being pregnant isn't the end of the world," she said, turning towards me. A tear rolled down my face. Yes, I was pregnant, and I was not keeping this baby.

"Desire, I appreciate your words, but this shit ain't happening. I have plans, and my life will go on as planned. I've been waiting for the longest to have something of mine, and with the salon opening in a few months, this shit is too soon. Plus, I'm already dealing with these raggedy ass hoes."

"Niara, if Nash ever finds out about this girl, he will kill both us. That man cares about you, and I can tell he does. I feel you should've told him, and at least let him have a say. That's all I'm saying." Desire sighed.

I had pumped myself up so that I wouldn't change my mind.

"Well, the only way he will find out is if you tell him, Desire. Please just support me on this. You were the only person I could confide in about this."

"Real shit, Niara, just because I brought you, doesn't mean I support you. That's still your child as well, and you're being selfish as hell about this. You know how many times a child has popped up in someone's life not planned. Hell, Ashton popped up right when Fiyah and I got serious, I sure as hell wasn't prepared to be a step mama. It ain't like you poor or struggling. You got support all the way around from everyone."

I heard everything Desire was saying, but my mind was made up.

"I'm ready to get this over with." I sighed, reaching for the door and opening it.

Walking towards Planned Parenthood, I had cleared my mind of all the thoughts that were plaguing it. I knew I was going to have to take this secret to my grave.

Walking in the place felt gloomy and depressing. I checked in and took my seat. I wasn't sure if Desire was going to come in or not, but I appreciate her for being my ride. I looked up, and Desire's ass came strolling in with some huge shades covering her face, and a damn scarf wrapped around her head. This hoe couldn't be serious. She looked around for me, and when we locked eyes, she came and took her seat.

"Bitch, are you serious right now?" I whispered.

"I don't need nobody seeing me and running back to tell Fiyah's ass they saw me at the clinic. He always knows what the fuck is going on out here before we know shit," she answered.

It was time for me to go back, and it was now or never. Standing up, I pushed myself and said a prayer. I just wanted this never to be brought up again. God, please forgive me.

CHAPTER 17

Niara

Four Years Later: 2019

This nigga had me so fucked up that I knew when I laid eyes on him, I was going to go off. When he looked up and saw my purple Bentley Coupe pulling up, he had better know I was coming with a vengeance. Nash and I had been together for four years now and married two. Our marriage had been a rollercoaster ride of happy times and not so happy times. Everyone on the outside looking in probably thought we had our shit together, but that was a gah damn lie. Don't get me wrong. I loved the fuck out of my husband, he gave me everything I ever wanted, took care of home, and all that, but he had his flaws as well as I.

Kima and I did open our salon, Diva's Emporium, the hottest thing in the Ville. Nash had gotten deeper in the streets due to him helping while Fiyah was gone, so I let that shit ride, and with that came the women and the lies. He swore up and down he was still faithful, but he just couldn't help entertaining women. Last night took the cake because not only did he come in at four a.m., but this nigga took a shower and left right back out and hasn't been answering my calls.

Nash wooed the fuck out of me when we first got together. He has never made me feel as if I had to even worry about another bitch, but for some reason, he just couldn't leave them hoes alone. There was no competition to me though. I was a boss bitch and all about my paper. The only thing I was not allowing any disrespect. He knew that he was in the streets heavy, so I guess him thinking marrying me would fix everything. Shit, the only thing changed was my last name, not his ass.

I turned down the street my uncle's studio was on, and I peeped Nash's truck in the parking lot. I made a quick turn whipping into the parking lot, blocking his truck in. Stepping out, I grabbed my shades and placed them on my face. Walking towards the door, I heard some commotion coming from the side of the building, so I decided to check it out. Peeping around the corner, I spotted everyone shooting dice. Nash was standing there as if he ain't have a care in the world. I hit that corner, and the sound of my heels could be heard because I was tearing the pavement up. They were all so caught up that they never heard me coming.

Walking right into the dice circle, I kicked the dice and money breaking that shit up.

"Bitch, the fuck is yo problem?" someone yelled. The next thing I know Nash foot went crashing into dude's face and blood came flying out of his mouth.

"Nigga, that's my motherfucking wife! Ain't no bitch in her blood!" Nash spat. Dude was holding his face and everyone else knew to shut the fuck up.

"Well, I'm glad you still remember who the fuck I am. Is there something wrong with your phone?" I asked, placing my hands on my hip. Nash grabbed me by the arm, walking me off from the crowd.

"A nigga don't answer his phone, and you come down here causing a scene and shit? Yo, you on some other shit," he had the nerve to say.

"You damn right I'm on some other shit. You come in at four in the morning, shower, and then leave. Where the fuck they doing that at?" I yelled.

"I got your stuff, Nash," some bitch's voice came floating past my ear.

Slightly turning my head, I locked eyes with a brown skin chick dressed to kill. The hoe was fierce I give her that. She held what looked to be some food in her hand. I done seen this hoe before, but I couldn't really place her face.

"Thanks, Mahlee," Nash said, grabbing the food. I knocked that shit out of his hand so fast.

"This you?" I asked, poking his forehead with my pointing finger. Nash hated that shit, and I could tell he was getting pissed.

"Strokez, man, come get her before I snap," he said through gritted teeth.

"You bet not fucking touch me."

Strokez shook his head.

"Niara, the bitch just ran and got everybody food and you sitting here tripping for no fucking reason!" he yelled.

Something hit me, and as if something ran through my body because I stopped. I wasn't a fool, nor was I exaggerating.

"Ok," I said calmly. Nash lifted his brow.

"Ok?"

"Yes, let me get out of here. I have to get to the salon," was all I said and walked off calm as fuck. Walking back to the car, I smiled because Nash was going to see me.

"NiNi!" Nash yelled. I opened the door and got in the car. Nash banged on the window, and I rolled it down.

"Nigga this ain't no damn pinto, break my window and you gone pay for it."

"I bought this shit. Listen, man. I just want you to know that I was telling the truth. I know things ain't been great, but I had to leave out and make sure everything is everything. Fiyah touches down in a couple of hours, and we're having a welcome home party tonight," Nash said.

"Well, damn. When were you going to tell me he was coming home? Desire ain't said shit."

"That's because she doesn't know. Look, just make sure you get her to Midtown tonight at nine, aite. I love you forever, girl, so stop thinking crazy shit," he said, leaning into the window placing a kiss on my lips. I kissed him back and didn't want to let go.

Watching him walk back, I saw that Mahlee chick get in her car. I was going to keep my eye on that bitch because I ain't trust her ass.

CHAPTER 18
Nash

Niara was crazy as a motherfucking red hen, but that's why I loved her ass. If you had of asked me, Nashville Palero, would I ever get married, the answer would've been hell no. Since Fiyah's been locked up, my load had tripled due to me helping Strokez and Desire. A nigga was twenty-eight years old, and shit, it was time to slow down, I was so glad Fiyah was coming home. I was ready for that family shit.

Niara seeing Mahlee sent her ass off to a place that I only had to experience once since Niara and I had been together. Now, I knew Niara well, and for her to be spazzing the way she was, then to cut that shit off like a switch, I knew it was hell coming behind it.

Our second year into dating before we got married, we were at Hadley Park for this community cookout that I throw every summer for the kids. Niara, Kima, and Desire were relaxing under the tent while some of my homies and I were chilling on our motorcycles and shit. A chick I used to mess with walked by and was on some flirting shit. I ain't want to be rude, so I knew to keep the conversation to a minimal. The only thing in Niara's mind was I wasn't even supposed to speak to the girl. The girl was walking in to hug me, and Niara had walked up going off. She spooked the hell out of ole gal, and she took off. The whole time I'm trying to explain to Niara and calm her down, and then she hit me with the ok.

My ass was thinking everything is everything shit cool.

About an hour later, I'm on stage about to introduce my homie that was about to perform, and I see smoke in the background. Niara was looking like Angela Bassett on *Waiting to Exhale* walking off after setting my damn custom royal blue and white Harley Street Glide with the 26-inch wheel on fire. My words were caught in my throat, and everyone started looking behind them, and Niara was standing there sipping on her drink as if she ain't did shit. So, I knew I had to watch her ass because she was plotting.

Mahlee wasn't shit to be concerned about though. I mean I done hit a few times in the past before we got married, but she's really been around most of the team.

Looking at my watch, I had about an hour to get to Fiyah for pick up. AB was being released as well, but Kima ass was all over that. She ain't want nobody picking his ass up, so I let her have that shit. Strokez walked over and handed me a blunt.

"Yo, Niara was about to go in your shit about Mahlee." He laughed. I just shook my head.

"Her ass is far from done. That hurricane was gone hit when I least expect it. I told her ass the truth. Ain't nobody checking for Mahlee's thot ass," I mumbled, and Strokez gave me this *nigga tell another lie* look.

"What nigga? Aite, I let her suck my dick, but that was it. A nigga really ain't been cheating like I used to since I got married." I sighed beating my own ass because I was lying like hell.

"I swear you niggas be dumb as hell. It ain't like Niara's your girlfriend. I think once you get married, that's a level of respect that should be sacred," Strokez came out and said.

This nigga had his nerve. He had hoes galore.

"Says the Hugh Hefner of the crew." I laughed.

"Nigga, I can be Hugh Hefner. I don't have a main bitch or a wife. I know my ass ain't ready to settle down." He shrugged.

"Man, nigga, come on so that I can go see my nigga. It's been a long time coming," I said, and we headed to the car.

My niggas laid down and took they charges with no complaints. They knew we bleed loyalty, and when they came home, things would be good. The drive to pick Fiyah up was about an hour outside of Nashville. My nigga had his blunt already rolled, a fresh ass outfit, and some shoes to lace his body with.

"I hope this nigga ready to get back to work. Desire's ass has been in beast mode. Don't get me wrong. She's good at running shit, but I think she done changed since Fiyah's been gone, and that shit that went down between my cousin and him, she ain't let that shit go," Strokez mentioned.

"That's a female. Lametrica's ass had better be lucky she's still breathing. I know that's your family, but Desire done killed motherfuckers for way less," I told Strokez.

I'm sure if he ain't know by now, she was a different breed, and a nigga prayed like hell she doesn't rub off on Niara.

After driving and running into a few bumps of traffic, we had made it. Pulling up, this nigga was already outside, standing there with his arms crossed and looking buff as hell. Parking the car, I rolled the window down.

"You waiting on an Uber?" I laughed. Fiyah bent down, grabbed his bag, and slowly walked to the car.

"Nigga, fuck both y'all late asses. Hell, I would've been better off calling a damn Uber!" he spat as I walked around the car and dapped my nigga up. I ain't gone front. A nigga missed my homie.

"We couldn't help the traffic, but shit, we here now. We got all your shit in the car, ready for you to get all the way right. Now let's hit the road, so we can get your ass back home and ready for this party tonight."

"Welcome home, nigga." Strokez dapped Fiyah up.

As soon as my nigga got in the car, I passed him the blunt, and he lit that shit immediately. All we needed was AB, and the crew was back in full force.

CHAPTER 19
Fiyah

It felt good than a motherfucker to be walking out of them gates. Four long ass years, and I was on the first thing smoking. Seeing my niggas and how they had everything set up for me was nothing but respect. I would do the same for them if it came down to it. Nash had changed his whole life around and stepped up to help Desire and Strokez maintain my business, and he didn't have to do that.

I couldn't wait to see my kids and my wife. When I married Desire, I knew she was the one that would hold me down through whatever. I was hoping like hell since I was home that things could just go back to the way they were, but deep down inside, I was prepared to lose a piece of my wife due to not keeping it real with her.

Once we got back to town, the first stop was to see my nigga JW so that he could get a nigga right. When I went in, they made a nigga cut all my hair off, so I had to grow my braids back out. A nigga's hair had grown out, and my face was looking like a damn werewolf. That shit was unsanitary.

Walking into the barbershop, the love felt was a high that a nigga could never forget. I dapped it up with a lot of homies that I knew from around the way. One thing about it a nigga was missed. While my nigga was cutting my hair, I was anticipating the party tonight. Desire was expecting me to be released Monday after next, but they let a nigga free early. So when she laid eyes on me tonight, she wasn't going to know how to act. The homie

AB was free, and we were finna take care of business. They could never keep a real one down for long.

JW turned the chair around once he finished up, and I took a look at my goatee and edge up. All I needed next was to go next door to get my hair plated up. While looking into the mirror, the door chimed and in walked this nigga with a little boy. I turned around in the chair and looked, and I knew he felt my gaze because we locked eyes. The nigga frowned up because he knew exactly who I was, and I knew exactly who the hell he was. With a funny ass smirk, he pulled the little boy towards the other side of the barbershop.

"Aite man, I appreciate it. You coming through tonight?" I asked him.

"Hell, yea you know I'm gone swing through. I don't usually do clubs, but for you, I'm in that thang," JW said, dapping me up.

"Bet," I told him, and I headed next door to get my hair right while I waited on Nash to get finished with his cut.

***

We stepped inside the club, and that bitch was crowded than a motherfucker. I knew this hoe had reached capacity. As I made my way through the crowd, I was hit continuously with daps and hugs. I felt like I had stopped and spoken to everybody that was up in there. It was all good seeing everybody, but my eyes wanted to see somebody else. Before I headed to VIP, I stopped at the DJ booth and hollered at the DJ. This weird vibe came over me as if somebody was watching me. I scanned the club to see if I could peep anything, and that's when our eyes met. She smiled at me, but I did not smile back at her. Matter of fact I felt myself get heated. I took a sip out of the bottle that I was carrying around and tried to remain calm. I knew she wanted me to say something to her, but I wasn't finna speak on shit while in this club.

"Y'all motherfuckers better recognize when realness hit the city. This nigga back like he never left, and tonight we going up for the homie Fiyah. Welcome home, nigga!" the DJ yelled into the mic, and the crowd roared.

After dapping him up, I made my way upstairs to the VIP section that overlooked the club and got lost in the music. Watching the crowd and everyone having a good time felt good. I noticed the crowd beneath me started to slowly part like the fucking Red Sea, and my eye landed on the baddest thing in that piece. She walked through the crowd, rocking a white blazer and a pair of black biking shorts. I don't know what this shit was she had on, but it looked like a gun holster, either way, it was on top of the blazer as if it was an attached accessory. She rocked a pair of black shades that covered the top half of her face looking like RoboCop.

Damn my bitch was bad. She looked up, and when her eyes landed on me, she looked as if she saw a ghost. She lifted her shades, and I nodded my head like yeah, it's me. She finally continued walking and made her way up to me.

CHAPTER 20
Desire

I was tired and irritable as hell as I sat in the chair letting Niara flat iron my hair. She was adamant about dragging me out tonight to a surprise party for someone she knew, and I wasn't feeling it but decided to go just to hush her up. Since Fiyah's been gone, my workload has tripled. I needed a whole extra person to complete all the things that I was doing on a daily. On top of making sure his businesses were kept running smoothly, I had to be a mother to our children, and that was the most important.

When Fiyah left, I was hurt and mad. I was already trying to deal with the infidelity then he gets locked up immediately after, so I had no chance to properly heal. Then on top of that, I needed Lametrica help, so I let her stay for another two months until she finally said she had another job and could no longer work for us. I hated the sight of that girl, so I didn't care much. Having to look at Lametrica every day knowing that she fucked my husband had me wanting to murder her. So when she left, that was more work for me to do. I had the help of the guys, but when I called the shots, it was still taking its toll.

Strokez and I had spent a lot of time together over the course of four years, and even though I could tell the physical attraction was there from the both of us, that was a line I wouldn't cross.

I was in the shop for a total of two hours. After Niara finished my hair, I rushed home to chill with the kids a little bit. I end up having to hire a babysitter for when I had to work late and couldn't attend to the kids, so she was going to keep them for me tonight. The kids and I watched a movie and had dinner together before I got them ready for bed. I took my time getting dressed even though I was finna be the baddest thing walking in there. See, with Fiyah gone, I know people thought we were going to fall off, and I was about to be walking around looking stressed out. Even though I was, a motherfucker would never tell when they laid eyes on me.

The ride to the club, I was smoking me some Sativa. I needed it so that I could be mellowed out. Niara was acting funny, and I didn't know what it was, but it was if she was prolonging getting us there like she was trying to make an entrance. When we finally got to the club, the line was wrapped around the building. I don't know who the fuck was having a party, but the city was out tonight. We pulled up into valet and hopped out the car. We didn't wait in lines, so we walked right up to the front and walked straight in with no search or nothing because we had it like that.

"I'm surprised Nash ain't been blowing you up!" I yelled over the music as we walked in the club.

"That's because he's probably in here, and if I see him with another bitch, we fighting." Niara laughed.

Niara loved the fuck out of Nash, but Nash wasn't taking their marriage serious. At first, he was, but he slowly was reverting to his old ways. That wasn't my business though. I had my own problems to worry about. The further we walked into the club, I immediately started processing the scene. I always paid attention to my surroundings. As we walked in, folks moved out the way when we walked through. I got this bad feeling in the pit of my stomach and looked up above me to the VIP I had to do a double-take because I knew my eyes weren't playing tricks on me. Lifting the shades I had on to get a better view, I was staring in the eyes of my husband. This nigga wasn't due to get out until another week. He winked his eyes at me.

"Surprise," Niara leaned over and whispered in my ear. I

looked at her like she was crazy.

I took off towards the stairs and was processing all kinds of shit in my head. Was I excited? Was I mad? I didn't know how to act.

When I made it upstairs, Fiyah stood there dressed in a tan Dickie suit with the shirt unbuttoned showcasing his tatted skin and jewelry. His hair was in huge plaits, and I must say he was looking edible as hell. Taking off my shades, we stood face to face, and it felt like the whole room grew silent when it didn't.

"Damn baby, I was expecting a better welcome than this. I mean this ain't visitation. A nigga's home Desire," Fiyah spoke.

"Why the fuck you ain't tell me you were getting out? When did you get out?" I started throwing questions at him. He began to laugh.

"Calm down, baby. I found out at the last minute, so I just wanted to surprise you. I just got out today, so no need to trip too hard. I'm home, and I missed you so much." Fiyah leaned in and placed his lips on mine, and I kissed him back.

"Bout damn time. Shit, I didn't think y'all were ever gone kiss." Nash clapped. I was so caught up in Fiyah that I didn't notice everybody else that was up here. Kima and AB were smiling, so I walked over to AB.

"Welcome home, big baby," I told him. That nigga had gotten a little buff.

"Sup sis, I see ain't much changed since I've been gone," he said.

"Not on my watch," I said. I reached and picked me a bottle off the table to fix me something to drink.

"Aw hell nah, who invited this bitch?" Niara hissed. I turned to see who she was talking to, and it was this chick I knew by Mahlee because she had a reputation like that.

"You got beef with Mahlee, sis?" I asked. Niara rolled her eyes and looked at me.

"I got a bad feeling about her and why she be all chummy with Nash. She was bringing him food today when I popped up at the studio."

"Aw hell nah, they friends?" I asked, pointing to Lametrica as she slid in behind Mahlee. I ain't seen this hoe in I know about two years, and why was she here and in our VIP section.

"Desire, stay cool. She's probably just with Mahlee. She most definitely ain't dumb enough to bring her ass up here in Fiyah's face after what happened," Niara said making a point, so I wasn't going to snap off.

I took a sip of my drink and walked back over to Fiyah. When I got to him, he wrapped his arms around my waist and placed his face in the crook of my neck.

"Damn, I missed you, girl. I can't wait to get your ass home. Matter of fact, a nigga finna dip off in one of these bathrooms," he whispered, causing me to wet my panties.

"I like the sound of that," I told him.

"Let's go," he said, pulling my arms so that we can walk out of VIP. We made our way towards the exit.

"Welcome home, Fiyah," Lametrica cooed a little too friendly for me. Fiyah hit her with a head nod and tried to walk past.

"Let that be the last time you disrespect me in my face. Don't ever fix your mouth to speak to this man again, especially in my presence!" I spat.

"It's a lot that goes on not in your presence," she had the nerve to say.

"The fuck you just say?" I asked, walking up on her.

"Come on, Desire. We not finna do this shit in here and not with her. She is *irrelevant*," he said, putting extra emphasis on irrelevant while looking at Lametrica in her eyes.

She didn't seem bothered or threatened with this ugly ass

smirk on her face. I jerked away from Fiyah and stormed out the VIP before I snapped.

CHAPTER 21
Lametrica

Boy had my life changed over the course of four years. When Fiyah got locked up, he had given me some money to hold me over because he knew Desire was going to fire my ass over our little fuck session. However, things got real, and she realized she needed my help to run that funeral home while she handled all his other shit. I only stayed there for two months until I got ill one day and had to be rushed to the emergency room.

That night I left the emergency room, I found out the fucking Plan B had failed like a motherfucker, and I was pregnant. To say at that moment my world started to crash was an understatement. I had mixed emotions about being pregnant because even though I called myself attracted to a married man, I respected how he treated me if that makes sense. We both were aware that what happened wouldn't happen again, and he looked out for me. At the time, I had started talking to this guy Mario, and he was accepting of the situation, so the select few that saw me thought that Mario was the father of my baby.

Once I told Strokez the truth, he told Fiyah. The wrath that came behind him finding out was terrible. He wanted me to get an abortion, but I wasn't feeling it. I looked at this as a sign because if it weren't meant to be, then the Plan B would've worked. After a few months, he finally gave in and added me to his visitation list. Throughout my entire pregnancy, I would see him on the days, mainly after a doctor visit to keep him updated. I knew for a fact that Desire didn't know shit about my baby, but it was only a matter of time if she kept fucking with me.

Fiyah and I had a three-year-old son that will be four soon. He made sure my son was taken care of by making sure Strokez laced me with money for Xavien. I wasn't a bitter baby mama, but I wasn't going to be kept a secret and continued to be disrespected. Even though I was with Mario, after birthing Xavien, my feelings for Fiyah increased. I ain't got no lie to tell.

Mario had taken Xavien to get a haircut, and when he came in, I wondered why he was in a bad mood. My heart skipped a beat when he told me that he saw Fiyah at the barbershop. Fiyah knew who Mario was well due to pictures, and Mario knew exactly who Fiyah was. When Fiyah found out I was pregnant, I told him that I was serious with someone and with him being married, he gave no fucks about my personal life. The only thing he didn't like was the fact that Xavien was calling Mario daddy.

Mario was all Xavien knew because I only took him to visit when he was a year old after Fiyah's ass had me served with a DNA test. When the test confirmed what I already knew, he demanded to see him in person. After that, he said he didn't want him back at the prison. What did he expect though? I just never understood that.

After our little spat, Mario left out pissed off, but he would get over it. I was on cloud nine with the news that I had received, but I wanted to know how long it would take for him to come see his child. Then God answered my prayers when my homegirl Mahlee called me. She overheard Nash talking about a welcome home party tonight, and she had all the info, so who wasn't finna show up and stir up a little drama?

That's exactly what I did when Desire came at me with that bullshit about speaking to Fiyah. I had to toy with her head, and when I told her it was a lot that went on when she wasn't around, I'm sure Fiyah would be getting no pussy tonight the way she stormed out the club. I just kept my smirk on my face.

CHAPTER 22
Niara

I wasn't expecting Desire to leave the club like she did, but I understood why. My girl hasn't fully healed, and hell, from what I knew, Fiyah only cheated once. Meanwhile, I'm sitting over here tryna hold my own marriage together with my own secrets and my husband's indiscretions. When Mahlee walked in, I didn't let her lose my sight when Nash wasn't around. I don't care what Nash said, something in my spirit didn't sit right with this hoe.

Kima walked over, and the glow she had about her was beautiful. Hell, she probably was the only one not dealing with a low down ass nigga.

"Why you mugging my brother like that now, what he do?" she asked.

"How about strolling in at four in the morning, me having to go find him because he left back out, and he wasn't answering my calls. Then that hoe right there has been in the mix. I don't trust her, and I'm slowly losing trust in your brother," I admitted to Kima.

Kima stuck out her lips as if she was pouting.

"I hate that I even brought you to his birthday back then. This is why I was against you guys' relationship because I knew what kind of guy my brother was. You are way too good for him, and it's gone hurt like hell when you get tired enough and see it for yourself. I'm not saying he is cheating because you know he stopped telling me shit when he knew I had your back, but our intuition be telling us the truth sometimes. I know that was why you did what you did a few weeks ago, even though you tried to tell me something different." Kima sighed, and she rubbed my shoulders because when she said that I held my head down in guilt.

"Just look at her, like there's all this space up here, and she's twerking all over there. He got me fucked up," I said and walked over to Nash.

"Why the fuck is she up in here?" I yelled over the music. Nash rolled his eyes and pulled me near him.

"It's a lot of motherfuckers up here that ain't supposed to be. Ain't nobody stutting her. She's having a good time like the rest of us. Now come here," he said, pulling me to his chest and turning me around to where my ass was against his dick.

We moved to the sounds of the music, but my eyes stayed on Mahlee. I smirked at her because she was burning a hole in me. I knew then she had been with my man.

***

Walking in the house, I removed my shoes at the door, and the effects of the liquor had kicked in. My head was spinning, and I was ready to fucking lay down. Nash was still in the garage, so I made my way upstairs so that I could get out of these clothes and shower. I hated the smell of smoke and remnants of being in the club because it lingered around. Turning the shower on, I pulled my hair in a ponytail and walked in. Closing my eyes, I let the water cascade down my body, letting peace settle in. That abruptly ended when Nash shouted my name. I didn't bother answering because I knew he would come into the bathroom.

"NiNi!" he yelled again then he rounded the corner.

I looked back over my shoulders and Nash had a dark look on his face. The same look that he had when I knew he was about to do damage in the streets.

"What?" I asked now lathering my body with soap.

"I was thinking, we been together four years and as many

times a nigga done nutted in you why you ain't got pregnant. You think we need to see a fertility doctor?" he asked and leaned against the doorframe with a perplexed look on his face.

Where in the hell did this baby talk come from all of sudden and why now?

"Ain't nothing wrong with me. Maybe you need to check your sperm," I answered casually.

"Get the fuck out the shower," he demanded. This nigga had me fucked up. I continued to do another round of lathering because I didn't feel clean.

"Niara motherfucking Palero, I'm on some serious shit right now," he said, walking towards me.

"This baby talk ain't that serious!" I yelled. He was starting to piss me off.

"Yes, the fuck it is when your ass has been sneaking to motherfucking abortion clinics!" he spat. My thoughts went to Kima, and I just know she better not had opened her fucking mouth.

Rinsing the soap off, I grabbed my towel and stepped out the shower, keeping my composure. I wasn't about to own up to a motherfucking thing.

"Ain't nobody been to no damn clinic," I replied, walking past him to the bedroom. He was on my heels.

"The fact that you lying to me right now is making me see you in a different light. Never would I have ever thought my wife was on some fuck shit!" he spat and pulled out his phone. Shoving the phone in my face, I swallowed the lump in my throat as I looked at the pictures of me at the damn clinic before and after my abortion. You can see me walking out, and Kima helping me in the car. Who in the fuck took these pictures?

"Who sent these?" was all I could say.

"Does it fucking matter? You and my own blood moving foul as fuck. I've been trying to get a baby out of you all these motherfucking years, and you done killed my motherfucking seed!" he yelled, grabbing me.

The tears started to roll down my face.

"All these motherfucking years and I've been trying to get a faithful man out of you, and you can't seem to do right for shit, but yet you want to bring a child into our failing marriage?" I yelled back, shoving him off me.

Nash placed his hands over his head, and he started to pace the floor.

"Hell, it probably was one of your bitches that sent you them pictures. I should've known from the jump the night I met you that you weren't shit. You know what else because at this point, I don't even give a fuck the shit is out. This ain't the first fucking abortion!" I yelled.

Nash eyes were bloodshot red, and he started walking up on me. I backed back until he had me in the corner.

"You better chose your words wisely, NiNi," he whispered.

It was now or never because he has yet to tell his truth and here it was everything was on me as if I was the only bad guy here. I pushed him in his chest so that I could get out the corner. I walked over to the dresser and grabbed me something to put on because after I say this shit might get real.

"On top of me getting pregnant when we first met, your nasty dick ass burnt me. You took my virginity and gave me a fucking STD. I should've taken all that shit in as signs, but you just wouldn't leave a bitch alone. How can you be ready for a family, and it's clear you not even ready for me? I knew you were only marrying me to try and show that you could be faithful, but you failed miserably." I sighed.

"NiNi, me cheating on you can't compare to killing my fucking seeds. That shit don't even go together. I could care less about the hoes I stick my dick in. I take care of you and home!" he spat.

"You take care of home, but you ain't did shit but break me. Do you know the way it fucking feels to know in my heart that you cheat and you constantly lying to me? It would be different if I didn't know about the shit, but your hoes just have to make it be known. Like I know you fucked that Mahlee chick didn't you?" I asked.

"I used to fuck her and good too. You're so pressed about Mahlee, and I only let her suck my dick recently." He shrugged.

"Motherfucker pressed? Oh ok, you just hurt right now, so I'm going to excuse that shit," I laughed.

"But I ain't excusing the fact that you killed my seed not one but fucking two. I ought to knock you in your shit, I done hit niggas for less," he said through gritted teeth.

"I wish the fuck you would, and I'll do it again because you know something, Nashville you ain't shit. The streets and loose pussy are all you ever loved," I seethed.

Nash came towards me like a raging bull, and I turned to run but tripped and fell. Nash grabbed me and turned me over on my back. It was like the pupils of his eyes had turned midnight black. At that moment I didn't know who I was looking at.

"I promise if you put your hands on me, I'm gone take you for everything you got," I said coldly.

Nash's blood was boiling. I could tell by the way his chest was heaving up and down. He balled his fists up and hit the floor beside my head, causing me to flinch. Nash pushed himself off me and headed out the bedroom door. I laid there looking at the ceiling as the tears ran down my face. I wasn't expecting for my world to come crashing down like this and tonight at that. When I heard a door slam, I jumped up and ran to the window. About a minute later, Nash was backing out the garage like a bat out of hell.

CHAPTER 23

Nash

Niara had me wanting to rock her ass, and I had never as long as I had been with her wanted to put my hands on her like I wanted to tonight. Yeah, a nigga had a problem with keeping my dick in my pants, but that didn't mean I didn't love my wife. Look, a nigga intended to change when I married her, but sometimes temptations get the best of me. All that shit don't amount to the pain she sent flying through a nigga. I think I would've wanted her to tell me she cheated on me with one of my niggas than to tell me she killed two of my kids.

I wanted a family bad as hell and just knowing that she did that shit out of spite because she was hurt, fucked with my mental. I grabbed the bottle of Henn that I had sitting in the seat and took a swig. I was already fucked up, but I needed something to numb this pain. I was expecting to come home fuck my wife good, then Mahlee sent me those damn pictures of NiNi and Kima walking out the clinic. You just wait until I see Kima. My own damn blood was keeping secrets from me. All these hoes were moving foul.

This shit here was a different type of pain. Don't nobody play Nash and get it away with it, not even my wife. I took another swig of the bottle before I pulled up at my destination. I sat there for a minute with my head spinning and emotions on ten. Pushing open the door, I stumbled out of the truck and walked up on the porch, laying on the doorbell.

"Nash, oh my god! What the hell?" Mahlee shrieked. I

pushed past her and walked to her couch.

"Yo, where the fuck you get them pictures of my wife?" I asked her.

The sinister smile that crept on her face let me know that my ass didn't need to come here anyway because she had a motive for everything.

"I took them myself. I happened to see them at the gas station, so I decided to follow them and your little wifey was up to no good." She smiled.

"You don't know shit because she could've been there for anything," I lied.

"Cut the shit, I was right because if I wasn't you wouldn't be here right now. So, what do you want?" She smiled as she ran her hands down her robe and eased it open, showing that she had nothing on underneath. Mahlee wasn't playing fair, and neither was I because I came here for a reason. I stood up and pointed to the couch.

"Bend over," was all I said.

Mahlee slithered out of her robe and bent over on the couch on all fours. With one swift motion, I dropped my pants and pulled my dick out. Sliding the condom from my pants, I slid the rubber on and was sliding in Mahlee's pussy. She was about to get some of this Henny dick. I didn't want to see her face or none of that. I wanted to buss this nut. With each thrust, all the shit with Niara and me kept floating around in a nigga's head. I closed my eyes trying to focus on the pussy, but the way Mahlee was screaming was irking a nigga. Now, I see why I haven't fucked her in a long time. She couldn't take the dick.

Flashes of the pictures of Niara walking out the clinic popped back in my head. Hearing her say she killed two instead of one like it was no big deal had me boiling. I reached into my pocket and pulled out my phone dialing Niara with a sinister grin on my face.

"What!" she yelled into the phone. I placed the phone on speaker and continue to fuck Mahlee like my life depended on it.

"What the fuck is my name?" I asked smacking Mahlee on the ass.

"Nash!" she yelled out.

"You don't want to give a nigga a baby NiNi, huh? Somebody's ready to take that spot. Ain't that right, Mahlee?" I asked while Niara was on speakerphone listening to everything.

"Mmm yess!" Mahlee moaned.

I let out a boisterous laugh and ended the call, powering my phone off, I shoved the phone back in my pocket and pulled my dick out. I didn't even bother finishing because that wasn't my motive.

"I didn't cum," Mahlee whined.

"Neither did I, your shit ain't hitting on nothing." I shrugged and pulled the condom off shoving that shit in my pocket. I pulled my pants up and headed towards the door.

"Oh, so I was just to get back at your bitch?" Mahlee sucked her teeth.

"Oh what you thought, you was gone take her place. You could never." I laughed and walked out the house.

CHAPTER 24
Desire

When I left the club, I didn't even bother going home. I took an Uber straight to the funeral home because we had a late shipment coming in tonight, and it made no sense to go home then have to come back out. With our funeral business, our people would pick up bodies all times of night, so shit looked discreet when we brought dummy coffins in. Strokez knew he had to be here, so I was expecting him.

I was sitting in my office, going over some funeral shit. The way these bodies were dropping in Nashville, we stayed slumped. The buzzing on my phone caught my attention, and I picked it up, seeing that it was Strokez calling me.

"Yeah." I sighed.

"Aye, I'm pulling up," he told me.

I pressed the button that unlocked the back door and waited for him to get in. I stood up and made my way around my desk. Still dressed in my club attire, I met him as he was walking down the hall.

"The fuck is that?" I asked. He was carrying a small box.

"Fiyah left this in Nash's car. I guess it's some of his shit." Strokez shrugged his shoulders.

"Aw ok," I said, signaling for him to place it on my desk.

Looking at the cameras our people were here, so we headed to the back for our shit. I stood off to the side as they unloaded the van and placed the caskets on the stands. Opening the casket, I felt around the filling until I felt what I was looking for. Removing the dope, I counted the casket I was on, and Strokez counted the other. Satisfied with our shit being correct and intact, we sent the others on their way.

"Can you take me home?" I asked Strokez.

"You know I got you," he nodded.

Making my way back to my office, I grabbed my purse and this box. Picking the box up it was rather light, so I sat it back down and removed the lid. Inside were Fiyah's items from jail like letters, pictures all that shit. A smile formed on my face as I looked at a few pictures that Fiyah and I had taken, including pictures of the kids. Combing through the envelopes, there were typical letters from Nash and me. I saw an envelope with my name on it, but the envelope was thicker than the rest, so I opened it, and several letters were inside. Pulling out the letters, I could tell it was a female writing him, so my eyes quickly diverted to the bottom of the letter and the name that I read immediately made me see red. Why in the fuck was Lametrica writing Fiyah? From the looks of it, she had been writing him like a motherfucker. I opened one letter and scanned it.

Dear Fiyah,

I am so sorry that things didn't work out. I don't know what happened because I did take a Plan B. The doctor said that sometimes they don't work.

My mouth flew open, and I dropped that letter in the box and scanned another one.

I am not getting an abortion because it's clear this child was meant to be here since the Plan B pill didn't take. That's fine if you want to be a deadbeat.

I was breathing so hard that I felt like I was about to start hyperventilating. The more letters I scanned Lametrica had a son by the name of Xavien that belonged to Fiyah. Combing through the rest of the box, I found a picture, and he looked just like Ashton and Ashlyn.

"You ready?" Strokez voice startled me.

When I turned to face him, I looked at him because he had to know what the fuck was going on this hoe was his cousin.

"Who is this?" I asked, shoving the picture in his face. The somber look of guilt consumed his face.

"I'm pretty sure you know who that is by now, and that's something you need to take up with your husband, Desire." Strokez sighed.

"Oh, trust and believe I'm gone take it up with him and your cousin, but you've been my partner for all these years, and you couldn't tell me this. I thought we were better than that!" I spat.

"Look, Desire. I kept my nose out of it. I don't want no problems because I fuck with all three of y'all, and I knew that shit was going to come out eventually." Strokez shrugged.

I didn't even have no words, because I was ready to get my ass to the house. I put all Fiyah shit back in the box and shut down my office for the night.

The entire drive home, I was thinking of a million and seven ways to kill my husband. Did I want to talk about this shit first then kill him? Did I want him to suffer? My thoughts were filled with anger, and all I felt was rage. I could feel Strokez every time he looked my way.

"What Strokez, dammit why you keep looking at me?" I snapped.

"Because I know how the fuck you get down, and I'm scared of what you might do, and I ain't even the one in trouble," he admitted, and I chuckled because it was funny.

"I'm still thinking about that," was all I said.

"Think about them kids, Desire." He looked over at me.

"My kids or your cousin's kid? I don't know who you're referring to," I said being smart.

"You got that, but you know damn well the kids that won't have a mama if she goes in here and hurt they daddy!" he snapped.

"Whatever," I sighed.

Strokez pulled in front of my house, and I grabbed my things along with the box and made my way in the house. Placing the box down at the front door, I looked over to the couch, and Fiyah was passed out snoring his ass off. The sight of him made my stomach hurt. I eased upstairs to the children's room and peeked in on them to make sure they were sleeping. They looked as if they didn't have a care in the world, yet my world was crumbling slowly like a soft ass cookie.

I walked to the guest room, and I could hear my babysitter on the phone, so I tapped lightly on the door. Peeking my head in, I smiled.

"Hey, I'm home you can head on out if you want or stay the night if you want." I smiled but prayed like hell that she took her ass home. Otherwise, I would have to hold off on my wrath.

"Oh child, thank you, but I got to head on home. My granddaughter is at the house, and I know she thinks I'm going to be gone all night. If you know what I'm saying," I smiled because I remember my teenage days.

"Yes, ma'am, I do. I'll walk you out," I told her as I headed back downstairs and waited on her to gather her things.

I stood over Fiyah as he slept peacefully. Imagining him lying inside his own casket, I wondered how in the fuck we got here because damn I thought we were better than this.

"He's been like that since he got home. I figured he partied hard. I know you are so thrilled to have your husband back home. When the kids wake in the morning, I can only imagine the look of excitement on their little faces." She smiled. I smiled back.

"Yes ma'am, boy are they in for a surprise. Well, you should get going," I smiled, trying to rush her the fuck out.

We walked to the door, and I watched her to her car. When she pulled off the fake smile that was etched on my face turned back to a mean mug. Walking back over to the couch, I removed the black bootie boots I had on. I undid my blazer jacket, folding it slightly and laying it on the couch. I stood there in my black bra and black biking shorts. Walking over to my bag, I retrieved my gun out of there and walked back over to Fiyah. I straddled him and he still didn't move. This piece of shit was out cold. Reaching back, I smacked his ass so hard, his eyes popped opened and landed on me.

"The fuck, Desire?" he said then smiled when he saw me in my bra.

I leaned down and placed my lips on his working my tongue inside of his mouth. Once his mouth was wide enough, I grabbed his chin while still kissing him. I then slowly eased the gun in his mouth and took that motherfucker off safety. His eyes widened. It wasn't much he could do with a gun shoved down his throat.

"I'm going to ask you a few questions, and all you need to do is nod your head. Do you love me?" I asked.

He nodded his head quickly.

"Do you love your family that you already have?" I asked, and even though he nodded his head, he closed his eyes.

"Open your fucking eyes. Do you love Xavien?" I asked.

He didn't move. Fiyah grabbed my wrists, and with pleading eyes, I understood he wanted to talk. I slowly pulled the gun out of his mouth.

"The only reason, I'm not tossing your ass through the fucking window is because my fucking kids are upstairs," he said low enough for the both of us to hear.

"The only reason I didn't blow you throat out the back of your head is because of my kids. How in the fuck could you do this to me?" I cried.

Fiyah tried reaching for my gun, but I moved my hand so that he couldn't get to it.

"Listen, if we're going to have this conversation then it will be the right way and not no damn weapons because I already want to smack the shit out of you for that dumb shit!" he snapped.

I eased off Fiyah and took a seat on the other end of the couch.

"I'm just trying to understand how in the hell did we end up here?" I sighed.

CHAPTER 25
Fiyah

A nigga was sleeping good as fuck until I felt like I got hit with something. I wasn't expecting to see Desire sitting on top of me half-naked. I was with the freaky shit until I was swallowing a motherfucking gun. Now, I knew my baby didn't have all her marbles, which is why I married her ass because she was down for whatever and she gave no fucks about having my back. I should've known the day would come when she turned that crazy on me, especially with this fucking Lametrica shit. How in the fuck did she find out about this anyway?

I ain't even finna front, but a nigga's life did flash before my eyes because sometimes Desire reacts before thinking, and I could tell she was ready to risk it all. Damn, I had hurt my baby, but this shit wasn't supposed to happen. A nigga shouldn't have ever stuck my dick in ole gal, and raw at that. The one damn time I step out on my wife this shit had fucked up my life.

"I'm just trying to understand how in the hell did we end up here?" Desire sighed.

"Desire, you talking like our marriage is over. This shit was not supposed to happen at all. Trust me. I know I wasn't supposed to ever fucking cheat, but that was a one and done thing. I wasn't even fucking around with ole gal like that, so if you heard anything, that shit ain't true," I stated.

"No nigga, I read. Your damn ass should've thrown all that shit away before you left the damn jail. Nah, you had to bring it home for a fucking keepsake, huh?" she snapped. I let out a deep breath.

"Well, if you read the letters, then you know that our conversations were nothing. They all were about Xavien. When I found out about that shit, I was pissed, and I wanted her to get an abortion. That shit didn't go as planned. So, she kept me updated about the pregnancy, and she let me know about her nigga she was seeing that was stepping up to the plate and shit. When she had him, I got a DNA test. Once I found out he was mine, she brought him to see me once after he turned one."

"This hoe was visiting you?" Desire spat.

"It was only to keep me updated on her doctor visits and to see him that one time."

"That's what the fuck a letter and phone call for. She ain't have to come see you. Damn, when was she visiting because I know I came to all my damn days? You so grimy, nigga!" Desire stood up.

"Sit down, man. Look, shit is real, and I know I fucked up, but I saw him today at the barbershop with her boyfriend. Seeing that nigga with my son did something to me. He's already calling that nigga daddy because that's all he knows, but I ain't the type that's finna allow that shit. We gone have to work some shit out and have a sit-down," I said, looking at Desire. Man, I might be tripping, but Desire was looking at me as if I had two heads.

"Who finna have to work some shit out?" She crossed her arms and rolled her neck.

"My nigga, us, you're my motherfucking wife, ain't you?" I snapped.

"Now you remember you had a wife. The very wife you had when you found out about this child and you should've said something to. You wait four motherfucking years to tell your WIFE that oh we need to work some shit out. Nigga, you been inhaling embalming fluid for way too long." She laughed.

"Something finna have to shake Desire because your ass

ain't going nowhere." I shrugged.

"You're right, I'm not going anywhere, but you are. You can get your keys, grab you some shit, hop in your truck, and get the fuck up out of here before my kids' wake," she had the nerve to say.

"Man bih, Desire you got me so fucked up right now."

"You had me fucked up letting that hoe talk slick to me at the club knowing that y'all had a whole kid together. She smirking and shit because she knows I ain't know shit. That shit is embarrassing, I'm supposed to be your fucking ride or die, and I'm blind than a motherfucker to the people in front of me playing games. Nigga, your entire life is in my hands with this operation. While you serving time, I was out here losing sleep, taking care of your shit and your kids. Peep this, do you know if you had of never cheated, you wouldn't have had to get up early the next morning to go clean your mess up. You would have had time to think about your moves like you normally do, but nall, you trying to go clean up your mess and that shit landed you in jail. See how pussy can be your downfall. So, like I said, you're going to get your shit and leave before my kids get up. Daddy ain't came home yet because I don't know who the fuck this man is standing in front of me. Matter of fact it's them or us. Goodbye!" Desire spat.

I know good and damn well this hoe ain't give me no damn ultimatum. I was about to wring her fucking neck, and I was going to leave so that she could cool off because this fool was tripping hard. I bumped her ass so hard when I walked by that she fell back on the couch, and I dared her ass to run up on me. This shit was so fucked up. I don't even remember what the pussy felt like to be dealing with all this shit.

I grabbed me some shit from upstairs, and I know I was supposed to leave, but I had to see my kids. I walked to their room and peeked at Ashton first. Damn, I missed my little nigga. Closing the door, I walked to my princess room, and she was knocked out. Damn, it felt like I had been away from them forever. Ashton was now eleven, and Ashlyn was six, and I had missed out on so much.

For Desire to fix her mouth and tell me to choose, and she knew how I felt about my kids, didn't sit right with me. I don't care what nobody says or who birthed my child, but that was my damn child, and it wasn't a deadbeat bone in my body. The same way I found out about Ashton and stepped up, I was going to do the same about Xavien.

Walking back downstairs, Desire sat on the couch, trying not to look at me.

"Since I'm back all that extra shit you were doing in regard to my operation, your services are no longer needed. You can just focus on the funeral home," I told her.

Desire held up her middle finger, and all I did was shake my head and left out.

CHAPTER 26
Kima

I was happy as hell that my man was finally home. Being away from him was the worst thing I had to endure, especially since we had just started to enjoy being around each other. The entire time he was gone, I put my all into my work and stayed at the salon working hella hours. To see Niara and our dreams come true was enough motivation to keep grinding harder for more. After the welcome home party, AB and I laid up in the house for two days fucking and loving each other.

Today was my first day back in the shop, and the energy was off. It was like as soon as I hit the door, I felt smothered. Looking around the salon, it was only another stylist and me there. Niara's station looked as if it hadn't been touched.

"Have you seen, Niara?" I asked Sandi. Niara and I stayed booked so for her station to be empty, something was off.

"She ain't been here in two days and canceled all her appointments," Sandi shrugged.

"She did what?" I mouthed not wanting to seem unprofessional.

I pulled my phone out and headed to my office. Dialing Niara number the phone rang, but she didn't answer. I then hung up and called Nash. This nigga's shit rang and then went to voicemail, I just know he didn't ignore me. I didn't know what the hell was going on, but I was about to find out.

Walking out the salon, I called Desire.

"Hello," she answered dryly. I looked at the phone.

"Um hey, have you talked to Niara?"

"She's right here," Desire responded flatly.

"Ok, where the fuck is right here and why hasn't she been to the salon in two days?" I was starting to get pissed.

"We are at her house, and you might as well come over here because she just called me over here," Desire told me.

"On the way," I said and headed to my brother's house.

***

I whipped up in the driveway so fast you would've thought a nigga died. Hopping out the car, I marched up to the front door and started knocking. Desire came to the door, and damn, she didn't look so good. She was rocking some tights and a shirt. When I walked in the house and rounded the corner, Niara was sitting on the couch buried underneath a blanket. It was empty wine bottles on the table.

"Ok, who the fuck died? Why the hell both y'all looking like you lost your best friends?" I asked, taking a seat on the chaise chair.

"Niara, you got me over here so yeah, what's up?" Desire mumbled.

"I'm filing for a divorce," Niara cried.

My mouth dropped, and I couldn't believe my ears. Desire shook her head and crossed her arms.

"What the fuck happened, I mean I know we had our convo in the club, but damn, I didn't know you were going to react this fast," I said.

"Hell, I didn't either. We came home, and your brother was acting weird. I'm minding my business and go take a shower this nigga busts up there talking about babies and shit." She sighed.

"Oh, shit," both Desire and I said in unison.

"Somebody, well I now know the somebody was Mahlee,

but this hoe took pictures of us walking out the abortion clinic and sent them to him. I tried lying at first, but the one with you helping me in the car gave it away."

"Wait a minute you had another abortion, Niara?" Desire snapped.

"That wasn't your first one?" I asked, shocked at what Desire said. Niara held her head down, showing her guilt.

"Kima I had an abortion when your brother and I first started messing around, Desire took me. Y'all I wasn't about to bring no kids in this shit, and I don't care what y'all think. This nigga stood in my face and basically admitted to cheating. Then he wanted to throw Mahlee in my face saying I was pressed about her and shit, but that ain't even the kicker. I know what I did may have hurt him, but y'all he went to that bitch's house and called me on speaker while fucking her. Talking about you won't have my kids, I know somebody that will." Niara busted out crying.

"Damn," was all I could get out. That shit was lower than low, and I could see him doing that shit to some random person but to his own wife.

"He ain't been back since. I have cried and fought with myself, and I know I was wrong, but the shit he did, I don't think I can forgive that. That was something he did to make sure he hurt me. So that means he doesn't want to work this out. So, in the morning, I'm filing for divorce," Niara said as she wiped her wet face.

"You sure this something you want to do though? Divorce is final. I mean do you even want him to work shit out seeing that he did that shit with Mahlee to hurt you?" I asked.

"I don't know. I just expected him to come home. Nash is never going to change. Apparently, I lack something that can keep him faithful to me. I should've left a long time ago. This just ain't where it's at." Niara sighed.

"Well, I might be heading down to the divorce office with

you," Desire blurted out. What the hell was going on with these niggas?

"I know you fucking lying! Your man just came home what could he possibly have done that quick?" I asked.

"Let's try having a three-year-old son by Lametrica," Desire nodded.

"This is way too much." I sighed and rubbed my temples.

"Oh, I'm so sorry, Desire." Niara leaned over and hugged Desire.

"Y'all know I thought about killing him, but my babies were upstairs. I was so mad because he had plenty of time to tell me this. He had me out here looking stupid, and this hoe walking around gloating and shit because she had one up on me. I found all the letters she wrote to him. She was going up there to visit him and everything even though he says it was strictly pertaining to the baby."

"Hell, is it his?" I asked. Desire nodded her head.

"He had a blood test. The baby looks just like the other kids. He claimed he told her to take a Plan B pill, she claims she did, but it didn't work. I want to kill both of them," Desire said. Her entire body was shaking.

"Well, at least y'all relationship is salvageable," Niara said.

"Fiyah's talking about he wanted to have a sit-down with all of us, and I told him them or us. He can't have both the fuck!" Desire snapped.

'I know you didn't tell that man to choose his damn kids, Desire. You're thinking like a bitter ass female now. Now, don't get me wrong. I swear, I understand your anger. You said Fiyah only talked to her regarding his child, which means he ain't worried about her. He can take care of his child without having to date her. That man wants his wife and kids plus one. If you were any kind of woman, you wouldn't even want to date a nigga who ain't take care of his kids. We don't date bum ass niggas. We date bosses.

How would you feel if say y'all get a divorce and his new chick be like you can't see your other kids once I have this baby? You would be ready to fight. As your best friend, I think a sit-down should happen, and rules should be discussed. Now, if she get disrespectful in the future, you know the bitter baby mama type, you can show out, but I really think long as he is dedicated to you that a divorce is a bit much," I told Desire.

She sat there with a smug look on her face.

"Yeah Desire making a man choose you or his kid is a bit much. Let him take care of his son and be the father that we know he can be to his kid. I know it already must bother him that he missed all that time from him. At least this was one cheating situation, unlike my friendly dick ass man." Niara chuckled.

"I can't believe that my ears have heard such things today. I don't even want to brag about AB and our situation. I do know that some shit about to come from this shit with Nash though and me taking you to get that abortion. I will never hear the end of it. Nevertheless, you know what ladies, both are you are very strong women, and even though you have endured this pain, I'm sure you have gained a lesson from it. Those lessons you will have to find out on your own. Niara, I'm not here to make you change your mind because you know how I've always felt about the situation. Desire, talk to your man," was all I said.

A bitch needed a drink. I wasn't expecting to come over here and be hit back to back with depressing ass news.

CHAPTER 27

Nash

Fiyah, AB, Strokez, and I were in the basement of the funeral home chopping it up, but my mind was on my wife. I hadn't been home since I left a few days ago, and honestly, I wasn't trying to go back after that shit I pulled because Niara was liable to have a damn bomb set up to explode once a nigga flick the light switch on. She was crazy like that.

We had the blunt in rotation, and all our asses were sitting here stuck.

"Y'all a nigga scared to go back home," I said.

"Nigga, not Nash!" AB busted out laughing.

"Man, fuck that shit. Y'all know that Niara had two fucking abortions since we've known each other and both were my fucking seeds!" I spat.

Damn, that shit still didn't sit right with me.

"Damn, my nigga," Strokez spoke.

"So you scared to go home because she had an abortion?" Fiyah quizzed.

"Hell nah, the shit I did afterwards. I fucked Mahlee on speakerphone and told Niara since she won't have my babies, hell somebody else would." I shrugged.

"Nigga, you so damn dumb. I'm surprised you even sitting here. You know Niara with that creep shit and gone sprang some shit on you when you least expect it," Strokez said.

"She can't do shit else to hurt me."

"Not that it excuses what she did, but what was her reason for doing it?" Fiyah asked.

"I can't seem to keep my dick in my pants. I don't cherish her or our marriage. I married her trying to prove a point and failed like a motherfucker," I said, trying to sound like NiNi.

"So, why do you keep cheating if you love your wife?" Fiyah had the nerve to ask.

"My nigga, why the fuck did you cheat on your wife?" I spat.

"Nigga, I cheated one motherfucking time out of the entire time we've been together. You keep on doing the shit before you got married and even after, so don't get mad at me because I asked you that shit. I was slightly fucked up, and shit happened. I don't know what to say about you," Fiyah leaned back in his chair.

"See, I don't have them problems because I know I ain't ready to be faithful to one bitch. I can do that though because I'm single. If I ever get married, I ain't stepping out. That defeats the purpose of taking vows, bruh. You niggas are always screaming out loyalty when both y'all dumb asses got some real ass women on ya team, and y'all fucking up. My nigga, I had to talk Desire ass out of murking you, so how that shit go?" Strokez asked, looking at Fiyah.

My ears perked up because I ain't even know shit was going down.

"Man woke up with a pistol in my damn mouth." Fiyah shook his head.

"Damnnn nigga, what you do?" I asked.

"She found out about the son I got with Lametrica," he replied.

"Nigga really, I thought you made that hoe take a Plan B pill?" AB jumped in.

"Watch it, nigga, that's still my cousin," Strokez spoke up.

"She did, but it didn't work. My little nigga three finna turn four next month— his name's Xavien. Desire's ass wild the fuck out and told me to pick between her and the kids or Xavien and his mama. The thing is I don't fuck with Lametrica like that. I'm only trying to be there for my son. That Mario nigga's been around my son since birth, and I don't like the fact that I missed out and now he's calling another nigga daddy. That shit is finna cease. If I got to choose, my kids are coming first. I ain't no deadbeat, and if Desire can't rock, then I guess it's a wrap for us," Fiyah shrugged.

"She's just mad. She ain't going nowhere. I wish I could say the same about my NiNi." I sighed.

Damn, I had fucked up. We both fucked up, and Niara was bullheaded, and I could tell she was tired of my shit. I was going to have a sit-down with her because we needed to talk, but I knew now was a tad early because that pain I caused was still fresh.

After we got done speaking on our problems, we filled Fiyah in on all that he needed to know so that he could get back to work. For me, that was less time in these streets, and time that I could focus on getting Niara back.

CHAPTER 28
Fiyah

After everyone had left, I had time to sit and think about everything that was discussed. I don't care how mad Desire was she was going to work this shit out. There was no way I was just going to let shit go willingly, even though she told me to pick. That's just not how I got down. Pulling out my phone, I slowly dialed the number and waited for a hello. Once I heard the voice, my body trembled as if it wanted to shut down.

"We need to talk," I stated.

After listening to a bunch of bullshit, I hung up the phone and turned on the retort before I headed out. Staring at the blaze, I missed this shit. It had been a minute since I burned a motherfucker up. That shit soothed my soul. Snapping out of my thoughts, I let out a deep sigh and headed out the spot to my truck.

On my drive over, thoughts of how badly I hurt my wife weighed heavily on my mind. The amount of pain I brought on her wasn't my intentions. That was one time I wish I would've kept my dick in my pants. A song I ain't heard in forever came on my shuffle list, and I shook my head at the irony. T.I. "I Still Luv You" came on I turned it up and nodded my head to the beat.

"Don't hate me shawty, but even if you hate me shawty. I still luv you," I rapped along with T.I. Damn that shit hits different now.

By the time the song came to an end, I had arrived at my destination. I could tell from the cars in the yard this might be longer than I expected. I grabbed my strap and placed it in the waist of my pants. Getting out the car, I walked up to the porch and knocked on the door. The door swung opened, and I had to laugh at this nigga, thinking he was hard— jerk ass.

"Lametrica is expecting me," I flat out said.

"Yeah, we expecting you, my nigga," Mario responded, giving me the once-over.

"I'm amused at you acting all hard, but my nigga, trust. You don't know me like you think you do, so let me in so that I can get the fuck away from here!" I snapped. Lametrica came from behind him and smiled.

"Hey, come in," she said. This nigga Mario was a joke on *Def Comedy Jam.*

I walked in and took a seat on the couch as the both of them went back and forth in the hallway, and I was already over this shit.

"Yeah, I got shit to do, so can y'all hold off on the family spat," I called out. They entered the room.

"You're on our time, so you need to respect what we got going on," this nigga had the nerve to say.

I was about to go in this nigga shit, so it was clear I had to regulate this meeting. I stood up and pulled my gun out.

"My nigga, I don't know where all this hostility is coming from that you got in your chest, but you need some Mucinex to break that shit down. I don't know if you think a nigga finna come in and steal your bitch or not, but all that shit is unnecessary. I'm here to set some shit straight and my gah damn son. So, sit the fuck down so we can handle this business!" I spat, checking this nigga.

Mario sat down and Lametrica I could tell she was scared because she knew how the fuck I rocked. I don't know why she didn't warn this nigga.

"Lametrica, you need to stop walking around this bitch fronting to everybody like we're more than what the fuck we are. Shit is plain as day. Xavien came from a one-time thing. You out here trying to disrespect my wife because of the secret we had, but she already knows. You out here with a whole nigga yet you're trying to make it seem like I'm fucking around with you. That shit will never happen. This shit gone rock the way it should be, and that's us being straight for Xavien's sake. Nothing more nothing less," I stated.

Mario looked at Lametrica like he was unaware of the shit she was doing, and she refused to look at him.

"My nigga, as a man I appreciate you for stepping up to the plate while I was gone, but one thing about me is I take care of my responsibilities, and I will be fully in my son life. He's gone know who his real daddy is. Hell, he'll probably be with me more than y'all. I got a lot of making up to do. Lametrica, you will have a sit-down with my wife to let her know the bullshit you were doing, on top of that, you owe her an apology."

"She has always come off disrespectful to me, I ain't kissing no ass!" Lametrica spat.

"That's because she knew your intentions since you been working for a nigga. You fucked her husband and rubbed that shit in her face on that messy shit, so she's got every right. I put on all my kids, you lucky that's all she did," I told her because we all know Desire's got a few bodies under her belt.

"I need more money," Lametrica called out.

"Need more money for what? You are already getting more than you should. I'm taking care of Xavien, not you and your nigga. Matter of fact, I'm dropping that shit from five grand to one a month. Anything you need for him, that's what I'm here for, so I'll take care of it. I think that's all I need. My nigga, can you go upstairs and get my son?" I told Mario.

Mario left out the room and headed upstairs to get my son.

"You didn't have to say all that shit in front of him. He didn't know about the money," this bitch had the nerve to say.

"Bitch, I don't give a fuck what he did and didn't know

about. That's what your ass get for being messy. Why in the hell should I come over here and make your home life easy breezy when you done fucked mine up. I told your ass to get an abortion, but I guess you thought having him was going to make me want your ass. That's probably why that nigga keeps mugging me and shit. I bet you told that nigga I wasn't doing shit for Xavien. You a grimy ass bitch, and I thought you were a real one, but I guess folks eventually show their true colors!" I spat.

Mario entered the room, and Xavien stood beside him. Looking at him made a nigga's heart smile. He was innocent in all of this, and I wouldn't dare walk out on my son.

"Xavien, that's your daddy," Mario told him, and Xavien's little eyes lit up. At first, I could tell he was skeptical to walk over to me. I bent down and opened my arms.

"Hey Xavien, can your daddy have a hug?" I asked, damn near choking up. He ran over to me, and I wrapped my arms around him and said a silent prayer.

"Be expecting a meeting in the next day or two with Desire," was all I said to Lametrica.

CHAPTER 29
Niara

The last few days had been spent finding myself all over again. Somewhere down the line, I had lost myself in my marriage. I'm not trying to say that the entire marriage was trash. It was just that I let more happen than I should have. I loved Nash with all my heart, and I tried to make this shit work, but it wasn't worth the pain anymore. I was more valuable than that. I deserved to be loved and respected because I was willing to give that to my man. Not once had I ever thought about stepping out on Nash, even when he did me wrong.

Nash had a lot of maturing to do, and the move he pulled with Mahlee proved my point. That was the final straw, and I had enough. I wasn't a bad wife. Yeah, I know I lied to him, but I did what I thought was right for me. Maybe I should've confided in my husband instead of being selfish, but he was selfish our entire marriage by not giving me all of him.

"Mrs. Palero, did you hear what I said?" my attorney asked me. I had blanked out for a second. I quickly looked up and nodded my head.

"Yes, I heard you," I reassured him. This motherfucker was fine as hell.

"Well, ok, then. I will get these filed, and since you wanted a rush, if you sit tight, I can get these to a processor in about an hour," he stated.

"Gone and handle that, you know I got you," my Uncle Rodney spoke up.

The attorney nodded his head and removed himself from the office. My uncle and I sat there in silence for a minute because this was actually happening.

"I mean it's a little late to ask if you sure about this, but I'm proud of you, baby girl." He smiled.

I was scared to tell my uncle what was going on between us, but I knew he had reach, and I had to tell somebody. My uncle kept his cool though, and that was shocking.

"In relationships, it takes you to let go without everyone else putting in their input. Nash is a tough cookie, and I know he loves you, but I just think marriage will never be for him. I've been around that boy since he was a youngin', and he never had a loving bone in his body, so to see y'all even make it this far was enough. I know you're going to leave a lasting impression on his heart, even if he is mad at you for what you did," my uncle said.

"I saw all the signs. Man, I sho understand the meaning of love is blind. You know what though. I'm keeping my last name," I smirked.

"You keeping Palero, you think that nigga gone allow that once you spring these papers on him?"

"Yep, I know way too much, and the amount of alimony I'm asking for he had better be happy with me keeping my name. I could be a dirty bitch, mention his secret accounts, and take him for everything, but money ain't shit to him. This right here gone hurt him more than anything," I told my uncle.

Call me stupid, but I had my own money, my family was straight, and our salon was top shit. I was leaving with my dignity and being free from all the pain Nash was causing.

***

An hour had passed, and I had an official copy in my hand, plus Nash was going to get served. I needed this copy for my dramatic exit because I'm sure he wasn't expecting it. Walking out of the office, I placed my shades on my face and looked at my uncle.

"Thank you for setting me up with your lawyer and helping me in this process." I leaned in and hugged him.

"Anything for you. Things might get a little rocky, but if you feel you can't handle yourself, you better call me," he demanded.

We parted ways, and I headed home. I prayed like hell that Nash wasn't here so that I could have time enough to finish packing the few things that I was taking with me. I didn't want much besides my clothes, seeing that I moved in with Nash in his home, so he could keep his shit. He could deal with keeping the memories. I needed to start fresh.

My place wouldn't be ready for a couple of days so I would be staying at the Westin for a couple of nights. I was able to find me a two-bedroom townhome that was for rent near my salon. I didn't need anything big since I was alone.

When I pulled up at home, the house was empty, and I was ready to get a move on. As soon as I walked in the house, I headed upstairs and turned the music on my phone on. I had been listening to K. Michelle's "Miss You, Goodbye" for the last few days on repeat. Reflecting on the times we had in this house was bittersweet. It was so many memories in this room alone that made my insides flutter just thinking about them, yet it was also so many nights that I cried in this room from being hurt.

I removed the last few boxes of shoes and placed them in the huge storage bin I had. Looking in the closet, my entire side was empty nothing, but hangers scattered throughout. I cut the light off and grabbed the bin and carried it downstairs, placing it by the door with the rest of the things I had packed up. Looking at all my things, this was the remainder of the shit I had left. Every day I was taking shit out of here and putting it in storage. That was all the damn clothes I had, and that shit made no sense.

Opening the door, I started to pack the things in my car, which took a total of three trips. Once finished I went back inside the house and walked towards the kitchen counter. I retrieved the papers that I had gotten from the attorney and placed them neatly there. Looking in my bag, I grabbed the sheet of paper that I had written a small note on.

I wish that you could change, but I don't think you can. I wish that you could feel this pain, so you could understand. I hate you're not the one.

Those were a part of the song that I had been listening to repeatedly. Placing the note beside the divorce papers, I looked down at my hand at my wedding ring. I should keep this shit, but it meant nothing to me. Just like our vows and marriage meant nothing to Nash, this carried no type of symbolic meaning, so I placed the ring on top of the paper, shedding my last tear.

Walking away, I headed towards the door. Reaching for the knob, I paused. Turning around, I gave one last look at the place that I had called home for four years. Turning off the lights, I opened the door and walked out. Locking the door, I pulled out the envelope I had placed the key inside, sliding it back through the mail slot in the door. Letting out a deep breath this was it. That was the end, well the beginning.

CHAPTER 30
Nash

A nigga was going home. Hell, it's been five days since my ass walked out that night on Niara. We both needed the space to clear our head and get our thoughts together. I had so much ass to kiss after that Mahlee stunt I pulled. Even though I was fucked up about the abortions, I was willing to let that shit ride because we could always have more kids, if her uterus weren't fucked up from being sucked on more than once. Damn, every time I thought of that shit, it pissed me off. I turned into our subdivision, and it was nice as fuck outside.

My neighbor was watering her grass, so I waved at the bitch, little white, snooty bitch. She always had her nose turned up at me but would talk to Niara. She'd better quit playing before I put this dick in her life, I could tell her old ass husband wasn't hitting it right. See damn, thinking about pussy again. This shit was finna be hard as hell. I pulled up and hit the garage button, noticing NiNi car wasn't there. Cool. That gives me a little time to set the mood in the house.

Entering the house through the garage, I walked in the kitchen, and something felt off as hell. I couldn't put my finger on it though. I stood there and looked around, then turned the light on. The house just felt eerily empty. My eyes landed on the counter and seeing NiNi's ring had my ass gliding over there like I was on ice.

"The fuck?" I said, picking the ring up.

When I saw the papers that sat beside it, my heart dropped

to my stomach. Niara was really trying to divorce a nigga. I tossed the papers across the counter where they went flying everywhere. The note with her handwriting I picked up.

I wish that you could change, but I don't think you can. I wish that you could feel this pain, so you could understand. I hate you're not the one.

~Love always, Niara

Hell no this shit wasn't happening. I went straight upstairs to our bedroom. Looking around the room, it looked as if nobody had been here. Walking over to the closet, when I turned the light on and saw her side was cleaned the fucked out, I got even madder. Rushing out the closet, I went to all her drawers and she had cleaned out everything that was once hers.

I plopped down on the bed and placed my head in my hands. This couldn't be life right now. I said I was gone to try and change. She had me so fucked up. I pulled out my phone and called her. The phone went straight to voicemail. I didn't even want to talk to my sister's ass, but I called her.

"Umm, what you want?" she answered.

"First off you're lucky you're my sister because I was about to call you out your name for that grimy ass shit you pulled and let Niara do. That shit was foul, and I thought we were supposed to be family Kima?" I spat.

"Look, did you call for a reason because this I don't want to hear. I wish the both of y'all would've listened to my ass and stayed away from each other. You dogged my friend out for years and that shit you pulled the other night with that hoe Mahlee was low of you. Now, what you want?"

"Have you talked to, Niara? I came home she done packed all of her shit and left divorce papers and her ring and shit."

"She really did that shit. Damn, nah I ain't talked to her." Kima giggled.

"What the fuck you mean she really did that shit? So, you knew she was about to leave a nigga? Man, fuck you, Kima!" I spat and hung up the phone.

The doorbell ringing caused me to hop up fast. Jogging down the steps, I looked out the peephole, and I ain't know this nigga.

"Who the fuck is you and why you on my doorstep?" I asked. The nigga looked like I probably done seen him in the streets or some shit in passing.

"Niara here?" he had the nerve to ask.

"My nigga, I don't know if you're trying to die today or not, but why are you on my step asking about my wife?"

"Oh, you Nash Palero?" He chuckled.

"Motherfucking right," I said, stepping to him.

"You've been served," he said, shoving the papers in my chest and running off.

Opening the papers, this shit was the same thing that Niara had left on the counter, but I guess since I got served, it's really real. I stormed back in the house, sliding on a damn envelope. Picking it up and looked inside, and it was the house key. Niara was playing games now, and she was about to see me. Looking in the kitchen drawer, I grabbed a pen and signed the papers. Getting my keys, I locked up the house and headed straight to that ass.

The first place I was stopping at was her shop. I didn't see her car out front, but I was finna go up in here to check. I folded the papers up and slid them in my back pocket as I entered the salon. Kima's eyes got so big when I stepped in the shop and stood there. Looking over at Niara station, someone was sitting in her chair, but she wasn't there. When I looked ahead, she was glued to her phone, walking back up front. Finally, she looked up, and when she saw me, she stopped.

"Nash, what are you doing here?" she whispered as she neared me.

"We need to talk and like right now," I demanded.

"I have a client. We don't have anything to talk about," she said, walking off.

I followed her to her station. I reached into my pocket, pulling out a wad of money, and peeled a hundred dollar bill off.

"I'm sorry ma'am, but an emergency has come up, and I really need to talk to my wife. I'll pay you for your time that you let me borrow her. It won't be long." I smiled to the girl who probably would've waited just if I asked her to because she was already drooling at the mouth.

"Sure go right ahead," she smiled and took the hundred-dollar bill.

"Let's go," I told Niara, and I moved so she could take the lead to the office. When we got in the office, I closed the door and locked it. Niara stood there with her arms crossed.

"Now, what do you want because you can't come to my place of business bringing your bullshit in here?" she spat.

"I've been to the house," was all I said.

"Well, then you should know that my mind is made up and no matter what you say, I'm leaving."

"We didn't even get to talk about this though, NiNi." I walked up to her.

"Yes we did, our conversation was loud and clear that you can never be faithful. It was so clear you let me hear you fucking another woman and brag about getting her pregnant. That was low for even you, Nash. I'm done." She sighed.

"You want these papers, NiNi?" I asked, holding the papers I signed up. She reached for them.

"No, no. I'll give you these papers if you let me have you one more time before we part ways." I smiled. Using my hand, I caressed the side of her face. Damn, I couldn't let this go.

"Niara, I love you more than anything. A nigga just can't get right. Did you know I never loved a woman before you? You gone give up on me now?" I asked.

Niara closed her eyes as she held my hand on her face.

"It's been four years, Nash. How much longer do you expect me to wait? Maybe marriage just isn't for us. We can still be friends because even after everything I still love you. I'd rather leave now instead of constantly getting hurt. I want to keep my last name though," she mumbled, looking at me.

"Oh, so you don't want to be married to a nigga, but you still want my last name. How in the hell does that work?" I asked because I was dying to know.

"Nash, I know everything about you and your business. You never know where life may take us. Nigga as much pain as you took me through, I earned that shit," she said.

I shook my head, no.

"Nah, you have to go back to Pines, baby. The last name goes with me. This ain't no Tina Turner or Andrea Kelly."

I was dead ass, even though it was cute that she wanted to keep that part of a nigga.

"Enough chit chat, let me hit that," I demanded.

I could tell she was hesitant as if she didn't want me to touch her. Placing my lips on hers, I kissed her soft lips. Then I pulled away and bit down on my lip, getting mad all over again. I turned Niara around and bent her over the desk. Lifting the long skirt she had on, I pulled them panties to the side and slid in. Damn, this shit felt good. Niara had another thing coming if she thought she was about to get rid of me this easy. I don't give a damn about no motherfucking papers. She was gone forever be my wife.

CHAPTER 31
Desire

Sitting at the table, my legs were shaking so fast, and I was trying not to cry in front of Fiyah. I missed him like crazy, but I was so stubborn because he and this child situation were eating up at me.

"Desire, I want to see my kids' man, but I'm not about to beg you to do so because we both know you not finna keep me from mine. Just like you tried to tell me to pick between them and Xavien, it's not about to happen," he spoke.

After I had time to process shit, I realized I was wrong telling him that, but I wasn't about to tell him that shit.

"Why did you call me here?" I asked, picking up the Long Island that sat in front of me and guzzled it down.

"Desire, this is me you are talking to. Look at me. The same nigga that pulled you out that fucked up situation with Kapp and your dope fiend ass mammy. You are my fucking Bonnie, and I can't and won't live my life without you. I can apologize to you every day until I take my last breath how sorry I am for the Lametrica situation. I fucked up and stepped outside of our marriage but only once. Xavien is here, and I want him apart of our lives.

Now, I invited Lametrica here because I had to set her and her nigga straight about a few things. Even though I had to show my ass because this nigga was under the impression that I was an ain't shit nigga. The hoe gone fix her mouth to tell me I shouldn't have mentioned the money in front of him because he ain't know.

I dropped her shit down as well and anything else he needs I'm gone handle that," Fiyah rambled off.

"So you just invited me here to tell me what I was going to do?"

"No, I'm trying to keep you filled in on everything because we ain't splitting up, so you can get that shit out your skull. I mean really, I want you to tell me the exact reason why you having a hard time with this. We passed the cheating part, ain't we?" he asked.

I let out a deep sigh and took a swig of my drink. I was trying to get drunk.

"I really never got the chance to heal from you cheating. You got locked up the next day, so I was immediately pulled into wife and work mode. I had to push all that to the back of my head while I rode your sentence out with you. I fought with myself trying to think of all the things I could have possibly done that would have made you run to another woman. Then you pop up in my face, and the first person I see was Lametrica rubbing that shit in. The fact that I have to deal with her was thrown on me because you never opened your mouth to tell me you had a kid. No matter how mad I would've been when you found out, I should've known as well. Now, I'm supposed to be accepting of him just because he's yours. That's a lot on me, Fiyah."

Fiyah leaned back in his chair and nodded his head.

"Here's your baby mama now," I mumbled with a smile. This hoe wasn't finna see me pissed off and give her the satisfaction.

Fiyah stood up and took a seat in the chair beside me.

"Where is Xavien?" he spat at her.

"He's at daycare," she said and sat down in front of us. I wanted to reach over this table and choke her ass with the strap of my purse.

"Aite so look. I called this meeting so that we could get everything squared away."

"My bad had to find parking?" Mario said as he walked up.

"My nigga, we already rapped. This was for my wife and Lametrica," Fiyah spoke with agitation.

Mario looked at me, and I rolled my eyes. He looked jerked the fuck out. I started to laugh.

"What's funny?" he asked.

"This shit is, my nigga. Either sit down and shut up or leave because you bout as irrelevant as your bitch!" I snapped. Fiyah's head snapped back like he was shocked. These Long Islands had me buzzed and feeling good. That nigga sat down though.

"Why y'all always snapping on people like motherfuckers scared of y'all? My son is not about to be around this crazy ass shit!" Lametrica spat. Fiyah opened his mouth, and I touched his arm.

"I got this. You know my son Ashton. I'm not his birth mother, but I've been raising him since he was five. Something happened to his mother. I would hate to have to raise yours as well because something happened to you. The one thing you can't play with is keeping my husband away from his child. That shit ain't gone fly period. You want respect. You give it. You have been disrespecting me since day one. I signed your motherfucking paychecks, and the whole time I knew you wanted my man. I'd been told his ass to let you go. Hoe, that sample of dick you got, you had better lock that shit in your memory bank because you will never get another. This is how this shit is gone rock though. How much are you giving her a month?" I looked at Fiyah who was sitting here eating this shit up.

"A thousand." He sighed.

My eyes got big because this child was about to turn four ain't no way in hell she needed a thousand a month.

"Do you want that $250 a week or the first of every month?" I turned back to Lametrica.

"The first," she smacked.

"You better make it last because you won't be getting any more than that. Now, whatever Fiyah decides to buy him that's on him, but we are not supporting you and your nigga. He looks like he lives off you. Also, there will be no money exchanged through cash or by hand. All your payments will be made through our accountant and with a check so that we can keep a paper trail. We'll have Xavien every other weekend, split holidays, and summers. I advise you to keep things strictly about your son when you contact my husband." I crossed my arms.

"First off, Fiyah makes way too much money to be dishing out just a grand a month. I know he does, and if I have to take him to court…"

"Desire, I think she gone be a problem?" Fiyah taunted.

"I know, right. I hope Strokez know your favorite color because I plan the best funerals," I said with a straight face. This hoe was threatening our livelihood, and I would go to great measures to protect mine.

"What daycare does Xavien attend because somebody is gone have to scoop him since his mama won't make it." Fiyah grimaced.

"Fine." Lametrica grabbed her purse.

"No, we're not done just yet. Why is it that you're so mad? Mario, I think you need to check your girl. You've been around all this time, and it's clear she got the hots for the wrong nigga." I laughed.

"Are we done because I need to go?" she asked. I already had that ass in check.

"You're dismissed. Aye, just remember you been warned. I stick to my threats. Keep that shit cute, and we can all get along just fine," I told her and shooed her away. Mario followed behind her like a lost puppy.

Picking up my drink, I finished it off.

"I take it I can come back home after all of that?" Fiyah

stretched his arms, placing them around me. I shook my head at his ass.

"You can come home, and we can take this thing slowly. If you ever cheat on me again, the next time I put a gun in your throat I'm gone blow that shit back," I told him.

Fiyah squinted his eyes and bit his lip.

"That shit got me on brick, and I ain't felt no pussy since I been out. My nigga, I'm finna fuck you in the worse way. Let's get the fuck up out of here." He jumped up and threw some money on the table.

It was like something in me clicked when I saw Lametrica, and I was not about to let her win. My marriage was important, and I knew that in order to forgive him, I had to be the bigger person in this entire situation. See, Fiyah's ass would've let her ass run him around in circles, so I had to put my foot down. As the woman of the house and as a mother, some rules and boundaries needed to be put in place. With her cousin Strokez working with us, I knew she knew way too much, so I had to shake her up so that she could keep quiet. I'm sure you know exactly how I am and let that hoe get out of order once, she was gone be cremated and placed in a necklace around her son's neck. Play with it if she wanted to.

CHAPTER 32
Niara

This was wrong on so many levels. I couldn't believe I let him do this shit. I ain't gone lie. It felt good as hell maybe because I knew this was the last time that we would take it there. Those final goodbyes be a motherfucker. He was trying his best to attack my pussy, but that shit just made me wetter. I couldn't believe how turned on he had me right now. With each stroke, I matched that shit by bouncing back on his dick. When I felt his hand reach around and started working my pussy, I damn near lost it.

"That shit feels good, don't it?" he asked, and I couldn't even respond like I wanted to.

Nash pulled out and picked my ass up, sliding right back inside of me. I wrapped my arms around his neck and rode the wave. This nigga hemmed my ass up against the wall and pictures were falling. Lord, I just knew my clients were getting an earful.

"Girl, you must be crazy if you think I'm bout to let this pussy go," he mouthed.

Just that quick, I was ready to nut and be done. You know how somebody says some shit and ruin the mood. Yep, that just happened. I wanted to scream out so bad, *nigga if my pussy was so good why in the hell were you steady cheating?*

I could feel Nash shit swelling up, and he pulled out and bent me back over the desk. Sliding inside, he grabbed my waist and went to work hitting my spot. The faster he stroked he was hitting my spot, and when he stuck his finger in my ass, I came all over his shit. The way he was holding me, I knew he had came as well.

Out of breath like hell, I pushed him off me and headed to the bathroom I had in my office to clean myself. Grabbing a damn towel that we used to dry heads with, I soaped it up and gave myself a little hoe wash.

"Aite, NiNi I'm out. I love you girl and your papers sitting on your desk!" Nash yelled out quick as hell. I heard the door close, and I finished washing up.

"Damn," was all I said because he bolted out of here fast.

Once I was done, I made my way back to my desk, picked up the papers, and flipped them to the back. This nigga had me so fucked up. I knew it was something behind the bullshit ass story he came in here telling. Nash was a hothead, and he was just way too calm for someone that was just served papers.

Walking to my door, I stuck my head out.

"Kima in my office please," I said and closed the door. Rubbing my temples, I kept staring at the papers. Kima walked in.

"Don't be calling me back to your fuck space." She turned her nose up.

"What the hell is a fuck space, Kima?" I asked, screwing my face up.

"This office space that you done fucked in. You just couldn't resist, could ya?"

"Ain't nothing wrong with no goodbye dick. Look at this shit," I told her, giving her the papers.

"Wow, so that shit is true. He called my ass going in about you had packed up all you shit. So you really divorcing my brother, huh?" Kima looked at me.

"Bitch, look at the damn paper!" I snapped, pointing to the line where Nash's signature was.

"Shit ok, crazy ass." Kima scanned the paper.

It read: *Haha, fuck you thought!*

"This nigga is playing games with me. Why the fuck couldn't he just sign the papers and let me be on my damn way!" I yelled.

Kima was bent over laughing, holding her stomach, and I didn't find any of this amusing.

"Girl he finna give you hell. He is not going down without a fight." Kima sighed.

"He gone sign them damn papers, watch what I tell you. Nash is trying to play these games and shit, but I'm not letting up. Everything I do from here on out is about me. I ain't settling for shit. If he loved me like he claims, then he would let me go. That's that selfish side of him coming out. He doesn't want me to move on and stop messing with him, but he can do as he pleases out here in these streets. He can take that shit to the next bitch because I've had enough. I need to get my ass out here and do my client's head before she starts with her shit," I voiced.

I folded the papers back up and placed them in my desk drawer.

"Take that shit to trial." Kima started rapping.

"Shut up, bitch. You keep joking and this shit ain't funny," I whined.

"Dammit, ok, fuck you thought!" she screamed and ran out of the office.

Nash was a big ass kid, and it was clear after all these years he took me as a joke. If Nash had cheated once like Fiyah, I could've worked through this and not reacted with a divorce, but this wasn't that. The one thing I wanted to avoid was a nasty divorce. My phone buzzed, and I grabbed it.

Hubby: *I apologize, but I can't let you go that easy.*

Me: *This is so unfair on so many levels. If you loved me, you would let me go.*

Hubby: *Look what you say.*

Me: *What are you holding on to tf?*

Hubby: *The only one I ever loved.*

Me: *Bye, Nash, you will be hearing from my attorney.*

I quickly put my phone back in my dress pocket and headed back to the floor.

EPILOGUE

Two Years Later

Niara

"Happy Birthday to you. Happy Birthday, Nash Jr. Happy Birthday to you!" everyone sang in unison. Nash held Jr. towards his cake so that he could blow out his candles.

"Yayy!" I clapped and kissed him on his cheek. Jr. clapped his hands as I started cutting pieces of his cake and handing him the first piece.

Jr. had turned two, and my how time had flown by. I stood off watching the kids' fuck they cake up and smiled at the happiness my son felt.

"That little nigga finna be bouncing off the wall all that damn cake and candy." Nash walked up shaking his head,

"Well, good thing it's your weekend because I don't have to deal with that." I laughed.

"You foul, what you got planned anyway?" He stood there and crossed his arms.

"Don't look at me like that, and last I checked I'm single, and I don't have to answer to you. You need to be worrying about Kimberly and not NiNi. Have you been treating her right? We know how you do," I asked.

"A nigga ain't gone lie. She cool and all, but she is boring as hell in the bedroom. It's like fucking a robot. You know a nigga got to have some shit that's gone keep me in the house." He laughed and covered his mouth because he already knew I was bout to go off.

"Nigga, good pussy won't keep you in the house nor tied down with one woman. If that were the case, we would still be together."

"Nah but forreal, I just want to thank you for being you. You never switched up on a nigga, even with us being divorced and shit."

"It's nothing, but I think you better go get your son. He's trying to fight on Kima's baby." I laughed, pointing at them. Nash turned around and shook his head but headed to him.

That day when Nash had my ass hemmed up in my office, I guess he was leaving me with a parting gift because I sho got pregnant. Once he found out, he really didn't want to divorce me then, but he came around, and after a year, he finally signed the papers. Our relationship now was perfect— co-parenting, and friends all on the up and up. As I said before, maybe we just weren't supposed to be married. As you can see, he still was running around cheating on his girlfriend, but that shit ain't my concern. Nash is an awesome father, and I wouldn't trade him for another. I'm happy with my life and the things that I'm doing. I'm even dating here and there, but no one has stolen my heart yet. My peace, time, and happiness are more valuable than pain.

Nash

The last two years of my life had been a whirlwind, but I was making it. The best thing that ever happened to me was my son. Ain't it crazy how a nigga was being petty and end up making a baby when Niara was leaving a nigga. I don't care though. The woman I was supposed to have kids with gave me my son, and I wasn't having any more unless she gave them to me. It was hard trying to let go because I wasn't ready, but since the divorce, shit was going smooth as hell. It was like Jr., and the divorce brought us closer. A nigga's finally been trying the relationship thing because at first, I wanted no parts of that shit.

It was hard being around NiNi because I still loved the fuck out of her. Maybe one day, not right now, but maybe we can get back together. It's nothing wrong with dreaming. Even through all of this, a nigga ain't changed much, but I can say that my son motivates me to want to do right by his mama. With that, I won't ruin what we have going on until I know my intentions are pure.

"Nigga, the fuck you over here daydreaming about?" Fiyah asked as he walked up.

"Life, I'm just thinking about shit. Where are your badass kids at?" I laughed.

"Man, nigga, Xavien was with Ashton and Ashlyn over there with Desire being bougie and shit. This shit nice though, I like how y'all pulled this shit together."

"I just paid for this shit. Niara's ass be doing all that extra shit." I shrugged.

AB and Strokez walked up, laughing and shit.

"My nigga you better teach your son to keep his hands off my daughter because Kayla hit his ass with a left hook." AB laughed.

"Hell nah, you need to get your child because she ain't nothing but a year old. The fuck she doing hitting on her cousin like that?" I spat.

Kima and AB had a daughter that was a year old. Seeing my sister as a mom was crazy, but she was the best at that shit. I guess you can say life's great for the most part. It'll be even greater when I get back Niara.

Desire

I watched as Fiyah stood off to the side with Nash, AB, and Strokez. Fiyah turned me on no matter what every time I saw that man. Things between us were back on track even though it was a little rocky in the beginning when we tried working through the

Xavien situation because Lametrica was really trying to play us out here. The nigga Mario she was dealing with cut her ass loose, so she tried her luck once since our sit-down, and it took me shooting her in her damn arm to get some act right.

Xavien grew on me, and he was the sweetest child. It's sad to believe he came out of his mama. That little boy loved the fuck out of me, and he called me Ma Desi like Ashton did. It's crazy how I wanted nothing to do with him, but now, I would kill a bitch about him.

I smiled as he ran around following his big brother. His relationship with his brother and sister was even better. They welcomed him with open arms.

"Wheww child, I'm tired and need a drink." Niara plopped down in the chair beside me.

"Who you telling? As soon as this wraps up, I'm ditching these kids and disappearing. Fiyah's ass finna be looking for me." I laughed.

"I ain't finna be looking for shit. You know I got that meeting at ten o'clock for a drop. So whatever you got planned, you better call the babysitter." He shrugged. I rolled my eyes.

"Why the fuck we got all these kids?" I said, throwing my hands up in the air.

"Aye, anybody got a bottle? My wife needs a drink!" Fiyah yelled out and bent down, trying to kiss me.

"Move 'for I shoot your ass."

"I think that's some shit you really want to do to a nigga because that's all you ever talk about. Just know that shit turns me on," Fiyah said and walked off.

Fiyah

Y'all finally got a nigga. I know I fucked up and disappointed those that love my wife and me. Shit happens and all marriages ain't perfect, even the ones that rock so well together. They just don't allow y'all to see that shit. I learned a valuable lesson though, and that was to never take my wife for granted because when I say she did shit for me that I know for a fact, the next bitch would've crumbled and left a nigga hanging. She was built differently. Desire Cole was built for me. My family meant everything to me. When I came home to them, it was a breath of fresh air. Even my baby mama was acting decent cause wifey had to hit her with that act right.

"Who the fuck you over here talking to?" Desire snapped walking up behind me.

"The readers, man, you know they love a nigga and shit." I laughed. Desire rolled her eyes.

"Well you tell them to stay they asses on the other side of that Kindle because this ain't what they want!" she spat. She was so damn jealous, and I loved that shit.

"I wasn't fronting when I told you I love you. Girl, you the only one that I wantttt!" I sang quoting the lyrics from NBA Youngboy's "Valuable Pain".

"Boy, whatever, bring your ass on. I'm ready to go!" Desire winked at me, and I knew what that meant.

Check it though if you want to read about how Desire and I came about then check out *Fiyah & Desire: Down to Ride for a Boss http://amzn.to/2EzyjXT*

The End!

KYEATE'S CATALOG

Games He Play: Di'mond & Kyng

A Savage and his Lady (Standalone)

Masking My Pain (Standalone)

Fiyah & Desire: Down to ride for a Boss (Standalone)

Securing the Bag and His Heart (Standalone)

Remnants (Novella)

5 Miles Until Empty (Novella)

Once Upon a Hood Love: A Nashville Fairytale (Novella)

Tricked: A Halloween Love Story (Novella)

Kali: The Counterfeit Queen (standalone)

My First Night with You: A BWWM Novella

Full Circle: Falling For a Cashville Boss (Standalone)

Mended: Pieces of Me (Standalone)

Taking A Thug's Love (Standalone)

Valuable Pain: Money, Lies & Heartbreak (standalone)

Eboneigh: A Boss Christmas Tale (novella)

Unsteady Love From A Thug (Series)

Unsteady love from a thug 2

Another Lifetime (Novella)

From A Distance (Novella)

The Take: Rag$ to Riche$ (Standalone)

Black-Hearted

Tricked: The Awakening (Novella)

Hustla's Holiday: Eze & SunJai (Novelette)

Return to Sender: A Sneaky Link Love Story (Standalone)

120 Hours (Series)

120 Hours Or Forever?